To my long ... to take this c ... you for all the

"It's a rare person who can take care of hearts while also taking care of business."

me all these years. You are a great friend.

Love Ya

Simply Teddy

SIMPLIFIED $ALES

TEDDY BEHRENDT

TABLE OF CONTENTS

ACKNOWLEDGMENTS

I would like to dedicate this book to my children and grandchildren. They have been such a blessing in my life.

But I write this book from my heart in memory of my Mom.

My faith and love of God kept me honest, fair and loving. I thank God for giving me the wisdom to put this into words.

I thank my grandson JT Adams for helping with the cover.

I want to thank my following mentors: Mike Henry (telemarketing sales) Lois Anderson and Sandi Hall (banking); Kurt and Cheryl Stutzke (restauranting).

I want to thank my friends for their moral support: I especially want to thank Lisa Novak, Brecken Haak and Janet DeJonge for listening and encouraging my original idea; Julie Dale, Judith Bell and Angel Burger for reading the draft and giving me innovative ideas and expressing their honest feedback.

I want to thank Jim Parker for moral support and his continuous pushing me to discipline myself to keep writing.

None of this could have been accomplished without God, my family and friends. I thank you all.

PERSONAL NOTE TO MY READERS

"I am what I am" ...Popeye

Dear Readers:

Allow me to begin with I am positive my ethnic upbringing and specifically my mom helped me to be the kind of servant and person I am. My mom worked at teaching me (and my brothers) to be happy and kind. She assured me if I studied hard, worked hard and worked fairly, I could accomplish whatever I wanted in life. I could be anything I wanted as long as I had a good attitude and was willing to listen and learn. I am sure this has helped me to get through the tough times as well as the good times. And we all have tough times. I know I have, but with God, my children, my parents, my friends and mentors I think I have made it.

I have been blessed with being able to make a successful living while being happy along the way. As I look back on my life I see that I had a pattern not only in my business life, but also in my personal life. No matter what type of job I have had, no matter where I lived, no matter who I met, I seemed to end up selling something and selling something well. Also no matter what type of job I had, no matter where I lived, and no matter who I met, I ended up with best friends. How fortunate for me.

I realize that I love life, I love the hearts of people and I love to serve. And this has flowed over into my selling. In my book, I am trying to tell you my secrets of success. I'll explain what did it for me. I am trying to help you to be the best you can be and make money while you are doing it. My philosophy has always been to take care of people and their hearts while taking care of business. This is a rare trait, but one that comes naturally to me. But I have no doubt that it can be learned.

I want to be completely honest, I wrote this book for me personally. It has always been a dream and I promised myself, as soon as I retired, I would write this book and now I have. (I will admit it has taken me over a year and it wasn't easy, but I did it). I want it to be used as a textbook or an outline to help you so you can sell more and be a better person while doing so.

If I help you with one thing in life, if I help you with one extra sale, if I help you feel better about yourself just once; then I will have accomplished what I set out to do. I start my book out with ***"If you always do what you always did, you will always get what you always got".*** So if you are not happy, make a change. This is a very effective thought. Think how you are today and what you want and then go for it, but consider the hearts along the way.

Thank you,

Teddy Behrendt
Teddy_berhendt_804@comcast.net

PROLOGUE

"Keep it Simple, Stupid or KISS"...Kelly Johnson

To me selling is a simple issue. To sell you must go to my definition.

My definition of sales: Listen to the customer, listen for the need, find the need, and meet the need. In other words hear what they want and sell it to them...it's that simple. This is nothing new, its what all the books say.

I have added two thoughts to this simple process. The first is that you have to help the customer – using a logical concise head – wanting the sale, wanting PROFIT but doing this with kind, but firm words. You need to be confident and strong and know what you are doing. You be a hard salesperson in your head, but a warm human with your mouth. Treat everyone the same and with kindness.

I called this my "Hard Head Soft Mouth Method".

The second thought is that you have to be able to balance all this with your head and mouth and become that "rare person who can deal with hearts while dealing with business". But you need to be very careful because there is a vast difference between putting your nose in other people's business and putting your heart in other people's problems.

This is the end of my secrets and the end of my process.   I always say when I'm done speaking... ."The End".   I will elaborate on all this but I promise you it is this simple.   So change the KISS from Keep It Simple Stupid, to Keep It Simple – Sell It.

Thus the name of my book is **SIMPLIFIED $ALES.**

IN THE BEGINNING

*"**God will continue to give you the same things 'til you get it right**"*...Anonymous

It all began when I was 26. My husband and I had just moved and I needed to work to help the family. Decided to sell makeup – never did before, but hey, give it a shot.

I was going to my second home show and I was very pregnant. I arrived and the young mother had a house full of women with her crying baby. He cried and cried. I finally asked if I could help and she said that he was hungry and they were out of milk and money. I gave her $10 and she sent her husband out for milk.

After the show, I was selling the kits. I decided to sell backwards. I offered the $175 kit and then the $150 kit. The women were so excited not to spend $175 that 8 of them bought the $150 kit. (I didn't even get to the $100 kit or the $75 kit when they started buying).

Anyway, at the end of the show, I explained to the young hostess that she had earned a $150 worth of free makeup. She said, "Great, but I also want to buy the $175 kit." I blurted out to her that since she didn't have enough money for milk that, in my heart, I could not sell her the kit. But then I said "Take your freebies tonight and as you get on your feet, I will sell you piece by piece the $175 kit." She agreed.

The next day I was at the main office very excited about my $1000 show. (This was before computers and we had to hand write orders). I was telling my boss about the young mother wanting the $175 kit and how, in my heart, I couldn't sell it. That very moment, my boss picked up the phone, called the young hostess and asked if she still wanted the $175 kit and if so, she would deliver it that afternoon. The young mother said, "Oh yes, I'll get the money from my mother and thank you."

My boss turned to me and said Life Lesson #1; "Women will buy makeup before milk. You just lost that sale, it's mine."

So I ask you readers? What's more important than milk? – Makeup or the sale. Answer: Both.

Thus, the start of my hard head thinking.

SIMPLIFIELD $ALES

By

Teddy Behrendt

"If you always do what you always did, you will always get what you always got." ...(Quote Lisa Novak gave me a few years ago and it has changed my life).

CHAPTER 1 - THE ONLY THING THAT IS CONSTANT IS CHANGE

I think it was in the 80's when it dawned on corporations as well as financial institutions to start to focus on a new concept and make some changes based on sales, and not just be order takers. The concern started with the industry making changes when Congress enacted the Competitive Equality Banking Act (1987) which allowed "non-bank" banks to proliferate and compete to a great extent with all financial institutions Deregulation caused more competition. Deregulation, as used by bankers, does not refer to the type of deregulation that freed commercial banks from government regulation. A disadvantage to the commercial banks is that merchants such as Sears, Insurance Companies, and Investment Services could now freely compete with banks, offering CD's, money markets and other bank products. However, banks continued to be restricted with insurance products. Unfair competition was in play. So banking had to change their methods to compete with the new regulations.

OK? This change caused all industries to think about how they ran their business. Unfortunately bankers still were thinking like order takers. And even though this new change applied mostly to the financial world, it started everyone thinking about how sales were being done throughout the system including the corporations and small business owners. It even affected the trucking industry and the loads they were hauling. Marketing became a new open field and marketers were hired to rethink the way the businesses were being advertised and run.

The new thinking was that we not only had to sell the PRODUCT but had to sell the BUSINESS and the COMPANY NAME as well. We began to see trends in the nation. Examples: Brand sourcing – All McDonalds started to look alike, all Wal-Marts were changed to be laid out the same no matter where they were located. You could, and still can, go into a Wal-Mart in France or one in a small town in America and know which aisle you can find the milk. Colors began to represent companies or buildings. Some malls even regulated the color of carpets for each store to coordinate. Howard Johnson's was known for their orange booths as well as their fried clams. The major banks started re-modeling so all their branches looked alike. Symbols became signs of certain companies, like the McDonald arches; the large cowboy at the IHOP restaurants. Mission statements started to use words that had "customer service" connotations in them like the Easy Button. ("That was easy") means Staples, "You're in Good Hands with All State". None of this was really new, just a different way of thinking – a new type of gimmick. Making sure that your company met the needs of the customer better than anyone else. That says it all.

But in order to accomplish this and sell too, there were new rules that had to be learned and needed to become a part of the sales procedure, to help the trained order takers to be retrained as salespeople.

Sales has been the name of the game since the beginning of restaurants, corporations, financial institutions, and any other business. But you couldn't say that – businesses were discreet about it. The word "sales" had the connotation of being a bad word.

And in a way, all types of business thought alike but differently. But everyone agreed on one thing. They wanted to sell what he or she had to offer. This again is not new. You see every company, every business, every salesman wants the same thing — PROFIT.

So the purpose of this book is to help you have what every American wants — PROFIT. And this doesn't just happen — it has to be learned. Sure some of us are more natural at it, but some of us have to learn how, but all of us can do it. In this book, I am going to train you, I am going to teach you and I am going to help you in whatever walk of life you have chosen to be the best salesperson you can be and make PROFIT for yourself and for your company. To do this, some changes have to be made.

"Think big and you'll be big"...my mother

CHAPTER 2 - CREDIBILITY IS THE NAME OF THE GAME

Before I begin this process, I need to make myself credible. My favorite book <u>The Radical Leap</u> by Steve Farber taught me that you must prove yourself first in order to be a teacher. So I plan to prove to you that I have the experience to help you. I know that I have to qualify myself as the expert so you believe me. I am convinced that I am good, but I need to convince you. The first realization is that is that it doesn't matter what you are doing in life, you still have to sell. And even if you say you hate selling, you still do it whether you know it or not. Some just do it better than others.

My Background

I started out in sales when I was 15 working at a Howard Johnson's as a waitress and had to sell the food. The more I sold, the better the tips and tips were the name of the game. But I learned quickly that good food and product were the small battle, I had to sell myself. The nicer I was, the more personable and sincere I was, the more tips I made. It was this very first job that I learned you also needed to have a heart as well as a system. Treat children special. Fill coffee cups with a smile.

Then there was the job of selling make-up in Terre Haute, IN. (You know parties at home with mothers who had little money, but loved make-up) The prettier I was, the happier I seemed, the more fun I had, the more make-up I sold – didn't take me long to figure out I had to sell myself in order to sell make-up. I was pregnant while working with make-up. My second largest party was with a young girl that had a 3-month-old baby boy and ran out of milk. She didn't have enough money to get milk. I gave her $10.00 to go get some. At the end of the show, when I presented my packages (I always did it the same, my system was to sell backwards and present the $175.00 package first, then $150.00 package.) The women were so happy not to have to pay $175.00; they bought the $150.00 package. To make a long story short, the young girl decided she wanted the $175.00 package, even though she already earned $150.00 worth free. It floored me, since I knew she didn't have $175.00. I discouraged her and talked her into only her free make-up she earned.

The next day when I went to the office to hand in the order, (before computers); I was excited since it was a $1000 show. I was telling the story to my boss when she said. "So you didn't sell her, then I will". She picked up the phone, called my hostess and promptly sold her the $175.00 package. You see when someone is sold and wants the product; it is not your job to talk them out of it. I remembered this forever. This was my first sales life lesson. Apparently makeup is more important than milk. Or the sale is more important than milk.

> *But I wanted balance, and I decided to think logically as well as use my heart. Thus my "hard head soft mouth" theory began and to do business with a heart as well. (My secret)*

From Terre Haute we moved to Hagerstown, Md. I was pregnant with my second daughter. I needed to work and help the family, so I started my own business in my home called "Myriad Business". My mission was to do anything extra any companies needed. It ballooned. I mailed 5000 letters every Monday for an SRA representative, I typed Masters and Doctoral dissertations, I corrected and filed real estate agents MLS books, I called customers for Insurance Agents. I placed women in positions for companies when someone was going on vacation or leave, (kind of like the temporary services of today, but on a much smaller scale). Within two years, I had 12 women working from their homes for me and two of them did nothing but babysit at a moments notice. I had one repetitive customer that decided he wanted me to setup his new insurance business. He ended up hiring me to manage his building that housed his real estate company, his trucking company and his new insurance company. He paid my way through insurance school (property casualty, life and health), so that he could have an extra agent. This eventually led to a full time position for me as the manager and agent. My home business slowly diminished and his business more than doubled. He never came to the building. He was a blind owner and we discussed all the business needs on the phone in the evenings. I took care of all the insurance business, adding new accounts, listening to customers needs and working with them to earn trust to acquire the entire family's insurance business. I wrote packages to include homes, car, life, business and health insurance; like a one stop insurance agency. I increased the book of business from 350 to 2010 in the 11 years I worked for him. During this time, my husband had returned to school and was working on his Ph D. He then took an internship in Las Vegas and we moved again. Another lesson: The owner went to work for himself. Three months later he sent me a letter saying he had no idea how much work I had done for him and thought he had grossly under paid me. Enclosed was a check for $5000. I called that a real motivation. I knew I worked hard, but being acknowledged was very healthy for me at that time in my life.

Las Vegas became a real experience for me. It was the beginning of my hard sales career and what I think sales is really all about. I knew my husband had a temporary contract for two years, and since I didn't have Nevada insurance licenses, I could not be an insurance agent. And life is not always easy.

I needed to get to work fast due to a health situation that caused a financial issue for the family. We were only there two days when I started looking for a part-time job and I saw this ad that said "Make lots of money with little time invested – Daily cash".

I laughed to myself but I had such a desperate need to make some money that I decided to check it out. It was a phone room that sold advertising products (pens, lighters and baseball caps) on the phone for 4 hours a day — commission only. Whatever you sold that day is how much you got paid. It was that simple. Four hours of cold calls. I thought I would try – if it didn't work out – I would at least stay at it until I could find something else. Well, I made it.

I'll get back to this job, because it was the one that taught me the most about sales, the most about hardcore sales, but I want to finish being credible.

I was fortunate in Las Vegas. I also worked a second job speaking at Harrah's Casino on sales techniques. And I taught an Incentive/Motivation Class, by Zig Ziglar "See You At the Top". This all helped.

Two years later, I went back into Insurance Sales when we moved to Illinois, Since I had to go back to school to get my Illinois licenses, I did sales consultant work. It was a whim of mine; I cold called on companies promising results and got hired. I trained Sears's clerks to sell insurance along with the washers and dryers. I trained newspaper ad sales people to increase their sales. I sold Polaroid pictures of home contents to be placed in family's safe deposit boxes in case of a fire. I typed dissertations again. Whatever it took, I did it to have enough money for the insurance classes. Then I passed the exams and got a brokered job for a large company in Robinson, IL. I was their first woman agent.

I only worked there one year when my husband had a chance for a better position in his line of work and we moved again. At that time I had accumulated over 2500 accounts. I felt defeated to have to start over, but yet I realized that I must have a quality that worked or I wouldn't have done so well in one year. It was a terrific year for me. I was named "top " agent of the year by Aetna. I was named "Woman of the Year" by ABWA.

I will explain that I attribute my success in Robinson to having a system.

I made fifteen calls a day with two cold calls being to outside businesses. I planned four hours a day in the office for existing clients and walk-ins and usually mornings so I was consistent. I had coffee in the same restaurant each morning, lunch at the little shops and conversation with the other customers whenever possible. I handed out pens and business cards to everyone I could and I was always probing, asking, and listening to hear opportunity. I brainstormed, did a lot of creative thinking and came up with the idea of selling all banks a blanket policy of foreclosed homes with Lloyds of London. Lloyd's is the world's leading insurance market providing specialist insurance services to businesses in over 200 countries and territories. It was a convenience the banks needed and a whole lot of business that I needed. They could add and subtract addresses with no extra paperwork while maintaining a constant premium. It was a need that was met and eventually five banks participated in the blanket policy. It was most lucrative for the banks, for the insurance company, for my broker and for me. PROFIT for all. I was convinced that I was setting up a fine business for life, but as fate would have it, my husband transferred again.

We moved to Sterling Illinois and I went into the banking world to work in the insurance division. But that was when the deregulation laws came into affect and I couldn't sell insurance in the bank – at least not at that time. So I started in the bookkeeping department and worked my way up to personal sales. Was promoted to sales trainer, and then branch manager adding on Investments and Insurances when it became legal. Fortunately I kept all my licenses into affect. I was in the first group of bankers to sell investments. So I continued and studied for my Series 6, 7 and 23. Now it is 22 years later and I am still in Sterling. I am retired from the banking industry. I grew the entire 22 years. I retired as Assistant Vice President, Branch Manager. I was known as " the trainer", "the sales guru" and "the cheerleader" – I was top in goals 14 years in a row in Investment Sales, and top Life Insurance sales for 3 years in a row. I had the record of achieving my quarterly goals, not all, but most of the time. The deal was when you made goals, you got a bonus and I loved bonuses. Great incentive. My goal was always to be #1 – it was not only a passion but also a demand upon myself. I always had a sense of pride. I would introduce myself as the Manager of "The Branch". Everyone was jealous that I labeled my bank. Sometimes they would say, "And I am manager of the other branch", but it didn't matter I had already established credibility.

My biggest accomplishment, however, was taking MY BRANCH from #54 (out of 68 banks) to #4 in the six years I managed. And although I didn't make it to #1, I still received the "ring of excellence" from the Corporate Bank. This was an honorable award, one I treasure and I am very proud.

"Give your best everyday" ...Zig Ziglar on Attitude

That's the most anyone can ask of you.

CHAPTER 3 - THE RULES

Now I need to get back to the <u>tele-marketing</u> job out of Las Vegas, because it is the one that continued to flow into my life and make a successful salesperson of me. I learned at this job that you needed self-esteem, self-discipline and self-confidence to make it and make it well. I know that I can do the same for you.

Imagine yourself in a room – glass all around and you in the middle office – offices all around with people on the phone and the manager is listening to all. All have the same pitch saying the same words and all being desperate to make money. It was a very nerve racking situation. So by using self-discipline and following the rules, following the pitch exactly, listening to the manager, and constantly calling, I made it – I sold and I sold. Soon I became the center manager and found out at that point it was my job to teach and train the others to sell. I was the one to give the positive reinforcement and to teach them that this really works.

I did well by following the pitch, following the rules and by using a system. I was always warm and kind in my voice and with my words no matter what. I seemed to do better than the others.

Maybe it was because I really cared about the customers and truly believed in the products. I called with my heart as well as my head. Maybe it was because I listened for the needs. Maybe it was because I admired the pit boss and maybe it was because I truly needed the money. Whatever it took I did to make this gruesome job work. And gruesome it was. Call after call after call. "Nos", "hang-ups", "rude people", all a part of it. But just hang up and re-dial, keep calling. Eventually a sale would be made and then another and then another. To keep my sanity I started tracking my calls. I counted my hang-ups, my pitches, etc. and my figures told me that on an average I had to make at least 10 cold calls, get to 7 pitches, complete at least 3 pitches and then I would sell 1. This seemed to help me. So I decided to make a chart on the others workers as well. I was fascinated at how much I learned and how this has helped me with training not only in a phone room, but also at the bank, in the restaurant, and even with my children. I noted the different type of sales procedures. Much of what I write today is from my notes of the trainings and sales positions I had in life. And I hope this helps you as much as it did me.

I learned so many secrets from this hard-cold call-selling job. But you have to apply them to make them work. Mike, the boss was constantly pushing. He butted into your conversation by feeding you words in your ear phone while your were speaking to a customer. Hard words, like "what's holding you back? Quantity or quality?" He continuously reminded you to stick to the pitch and never ask a question that could be answered with the word "no". And my favorite (which I used all the time), you TELL them what you are doing, don't' ask. Example: " OK, you win, .78 cents is too much for you so I'll send you 100 pens at .68 cents each with your logo and if you are happy then you call me back for the next order. FAIR ENOUGH? And your company logo is State Farm, correct? I have it so that makes it easy for both of us. I know you are now happy, so they are on their way in the next two days (head) and let me take the time to thank you for your business". (heart) I know you will be happy with these. When you get down to around 10 just give me a call. I will keep all your records handy.

THIS IS HARD CORE SALES. ***THE BIG SECRET IS TO ALWAYS FINISH WITH A FACT...and then soften down from the heart.***

Soon I was sent to South Dakota to setup and train for a second phone room selling computer discs. All the while, I thought this was great fun.

I feel compelled to tell you some of the things that I learned at this gruesome job and I stress to you that these are the rules that I followed to make this work for me and if you do heed them they will work for you. I promise.

RULE 1 - GET UP EARLY

Lay awake in your bed and think for five minutes before you put your feet on the ground. Organize your thoughts and your day. Decide on what you can worry about and what really isn't a worry at least not for today. Put time on worry. If it can't be taken care of today, why waste timing worrying about it. Decide what you want to accomplish and then get up and dismiss what you shouldn't worry about and what you can't accomplish. Decide what needs to be done and get to it. Of course there are always things that happen that isn't in your plan, but this kind of thinking gives you a basis, a handle, something you can grip. It causes confidence so that you can get through your day with a good feeling. Example I decide in my head that each child needs $2.00 for lunches and I have the dollar bills in my purse. I get up to find out my husband needs $4.00 also, I don't have that many dollars, so off to the store to get change before I even begin my day — but a smile and early up helps through this small moment. It doesn't have to cause a scene or be an event. Just do it.

RULE 2 - DRESS FOR SUCCESS

Everyone knows this and acts like they do this, but they don't do it. Dress carefully and for success. If you look messy no one believes in you. You don't have to be rich to look nice, but you do have to be clean. And ironing is a must. It's the whole picture that counts. It will make you feel better and if you feel better it is easier to give your best.

RULE 3 - ELIMINATE THE
NEGATIVE AND GO POSITIVE

Change every situation in your mind to a positive feeling. This is not easy –you have to force it and soon it becomes a habit. It is easier to be down. Believe me I know. We all have down times and so do I, but all you can ask for is for someone to listen a minute, give you some time to think it out and then start again. Sometimes a little love can turn it around or a smile or just a look. In Las Vegas when I had to create the happiness, I wore my actor's hat a lot and my smile. Of course, my workers at this job were NOT excited about making cold calls for four hours and how CAN that make you happy. So developing positive feelings was an absolute necessity. There were so many personal problems with each worker and this all carried to the job. If they were sad or angry, it usually showed and could be heard on the phone. As a supervisor, you must care. I had to listen and find out what their REAL problem was – give them five minutes to vent, then tell them "OK" that's done, let's get on with making money. Then smile, because all we really want is PROFIT. This kind of thinking becomes contagious and feeds to each other. Soon you are not the only one solving the negatives. The co-workers are buddies and all care and listen to each other, and that quickly carries over to caring and listening to the customers. I had a note on my desk that said:

"Be kind to everyone, you don't know what's happening in their life today".

It kept me humble.

17

In order to make sales, you have to help each other. I'll tell you a story about one of the girls at the "boiler shop" (as we called it). She could not make a sale. She always sounded sad and desperate. I sat with her and listening for her need with my heart, I learned she had a handicap child at home and worrying about him was what was occupying her head. He was only nine and needed her. I made a deal with her. With each sale she made, she earned the right to call her son and if she made 3 sales, she could go home early. I would still pay her for four hours. This was the incentive she needed to motivate her to start to smile and sell with confidence. From that day forward, she usually had her 3 sales made by the first two hours, so she could go home. She told me she was "blessed" to have the deal. It turned out to be a win/win situation.

RULE 4 - BE HAPPY

You cannot carry your worries with you; leave them at home or in the car. Put a time on worry – it works. EX: If your son has the car and he says he will be home at 11:00 pm, don't waste your evening worrying. He will not come home early. Say, (in your head) if John is not back with the car at 11:05 pm, then I am allowed to worry. More often than not, John will be home on time. This saves anxiety.

Remember happiness is a habit. When you get up in the morning you must decide it is a new day — You cannot look at yesterday and feel badly.

"If you continue to look at yesterday, you will lose tomorrow"... Author Unknown

No one in the business world knows or even cares what happened to you yesterday. It is all brand new today. If you keep looking back it's like driving forward while you are looking in the rear view mirror. It doesn't work.

My mom once told me, "If you act happy you'll be happy. If you think you can handle it, then you will handle it. If you wear an actor's hat it will soon be natural and then your habits are good." I know that some of this is how you were raised. You see in my home, my mom had this thing about everyone coming downstairs with a smile on his or her face. She was often singing "Oh what a beautiful morning" - actually it was a bit annoying, but it did make you smile, cause she couldn't sing.

Anyway, the point is if we were not happy, she simply sent us back to our rooms. Told us to stay there until we could deal with life – she didn't care if we were going to be late, if we had a stomach ache – she just cared that we were happy and starting a new day fresh. She would say "if you can't handle it today, then stay there until you can". I will admit to you that our morning breakfasts were pretty pleasant. Don't get me wrong, my Mom allowed us to be sad and vent, but she truly believed that you shouldn't take a bad moment and let it ruin your hour or take a bad hour and let it ruin or rule your day. Nor did she allow you to let one bad day ruin your week. My mother had the philosophy that no matter what happens today, – the sun will come up tomorrow and it will be a new day – a new start.

"A smile is a curve that can straighten out a lot of things"...Shakespeare

I have a personal secret about being happy, I will share it with you. When I am down I tell myself, I've been a good woman

> a good mother
> a good insurance agent
> a good banker
> a good waitress
> a good friend
> a good salesperson
> and I am me.

And in all this aspects I have been successful and given my best, therefore, I am happy. And since everyone deserves five minutes of happiness a day, I think I'll take mine now.

You know, life can be fun...take inventory, find your fun and go for it.

Trust me, all this applies to being the best salesperson you can be. Because sales is conversation with a good attitude and conversation is a part of life. That means if you have a good attitude, your motivation will be good as well.

RULE 5 - THINK OF YOURSELF AS A SALESPERSON

Think of yourself as a successful sales person. "THINK BIG AND YOU'LL BE BIG". (Another quote by my Mom).

This entire sales manual is to help you develop a sales image and less of a "typical" order taker image. It's how we perceive ourselves. It's a learned process that soon will flow automatically. You think like a salesman, but continue to act like a normal human worker. You will soon learn the needs of the customers, what products they are looking for, their sales paths and some of their personal traits. This can happen and you will be surprised at how easily it comes together. The main thought process is to consider the customer. This is simple.

Listen to the customer, listen for the need, find the need and sell it all with a smile.
THAT'S IT.

Write this down and post it somewhere.

RULE 6 - LIFE IS A SYSTEM

We can't get away from it. I have and will be saying I used a system throughout the book, but I really believe this. Life is a system, church is a system, school is a system, family is a system...sales is a system. Your business is YOUR system. Know it and apply it. It works.

What exactly is a system?
A system is figuring out what works
and doing it the same way every time.

I learned this lesson when I was pregnant with my 3rd child and went to visit my Sitto (Grandmother in Syrian). She was 96 years of age and I went to learn how to cook some Syrian foods. My mother had died and I missed her.

My "Sitto" was cooking. In her home breakfast was at 6am, lunch at noon, and dinner at 6pm. House was clean, laundry was done, my grandfather was happy. She had raised 7 daughters and the house was buzzing with grandchildren and great-grandchildren. I asked "How do you get it all done?" "Honey," she said, "I have a system, it's my secret. I found the meals everyone likes, and I make them the same every time. I make coffee the same, I grocery shop with a list. It makes life so much easier. I had to decide years ago to enjoy the house, the cooking and the family. Your grandfather WILL NOT go out to eat and since I love him and he is the one I need to please, I decided to enjoy it. It is up to me to keep this home happy. THAT IS MY JOB. Systems work honey, so get used to it." And so I did and I do.

That's when I began to think about life and how it really is all a system. At church I sit in the same pew. At the bank, I set my desk up the same way each morning. At the restaurant we set the tables the same way. Glass at the top of the knife, napkin in the middle, and prepare the salads the same each time, etc. I write my checks out, all the bills on one day. I make my bed the same. This works. So when you are in your office, decide what works for you, set it up and don't change that. It's a time saver, a decision-making saver. Apply it to your daily work habits. Treat the customers the same, treat your employees and co-workers the same. TRUST ME THIS WORKS. You see life IS a system. Churches run with a system, schools run with a system, corporations run on a system and so should SALES.

Remember my grandmother's words and apply them. You have to work, you have to eat, and you need to please many people. So decide to enjoy it. **It is your job. Yes, systems work.**

To help you a little more with having a system, I need to refer to all the experts that I have read. They agree on at least one rule when it comes to having a system. And that is the rule on time management of **"Do it now!** But tackling assignments right now is not always as easy as it sounds. You may be overwhelmed with the size of the job or with the goal requirements. Or you may not be in the mood today to sell or even finish the paper work of your last sale. This causes you to put off what needs to be done. You will then have to search for determination to forge ahead, to discipline yourself to stay on track. Otherwise you will find yourself procrastinating and drifting causing wasted time or procrastination.

RULE 7 - DON'T PROCRASTINATE

To procrastinate means to put off doing a task – for no good reason. The last phrase "for no good reason", is important because there are times when you have to put off a certain task to do another first. That's prioritizing.

But sometimes you put off a task simply because it is something unpleasant and you just don't want to do it. You will then have to convince yourself the task is worth doing, even if it's hard to get started. Once started, you might even be surprised at how good you feel especially when it is completed. That's called persuading yourself to do the task. If you have a system, this will become even easier. You have to "just do it".

There is help with procrastination. You can try to do the following:

1.   Put important papers in a red folder. This will be a reminder to do these first

2.   Make a "to do" list of what you want to accomplish today.

3.   Break big jobs into small pieces and complete one piece each day. Example: If you need to write a report, outline it today and put it into paragraphs tomorrow. It will be less painful.

4.   Discipline yourself for five minutes. Set a timer, when the timer goes off, decide if you want to work another five minutes on that project or if you want to move on to another. Often starting the project is the hardest part, but once you make that jump into the pool and start swimming, it feels good and you don't want to get out. This is the same theory.

5.   Schedule a routine (a system). Make your return phone calls at a certain time in the morning and answer your emails right after lunch.

These are just a few things that can help you to not procrastinate and help you to create your own systems to make your job easier and more productive. Spend some time thinking about this and determine what works for you and just do it.

RULE 8 - A CUSTOMER IS BUSINESS, NOT AN INTRUSION

I know you have heard this a thousand times, but somehow, customers don't think you have. Besides, lack of smiling and happiness, this is the #1 complaint customers have. They feel like they have interrupted you. Customers are offended easily. If you are on the phone with business and don't acknowledge them, they think you are rude. If you don't smile and just indicate with a finger you'll be with them in a minute, they think you are ignoring them. But if you smile and nod, they will be happy to wait. So I developed a <u>system</u> of trying to treat customers like they were coming into my home, think with my heart as well as my head and then remember they are business, so when it is their turn you can sell them. We all need the money and they came to see you, have a soft mouth but in the back of your head you think profit.

Throughout this manual, I will help you learn to listen for the need, probe, question and decide the sale by holding a normal conversation. The customer won't even know what happened or how it happened; yet they will end up happy. Most of my customers thanked me for caring. In fact I have been retired almost two years now and I still get calls just to say hello because they think I cared (and I did and I do). The hard head soft mouth method.

**"Every Customer - Every Time – Everything Counts – Everybody Plays the same Fairly"...
Arthur Unknown**

At the same time, we all work for the company, so loyalty and commitment will enter into this. You need to listen for the needs and relate to the customer in order to give them the correct product or service and they will be completely satisfied.

REMEMBER: It is your job to be NICE – sell yourself, help the customer, and sell your company as well as the product. Product is easy — you are the hard one to sell. I'll get more specific as we get into product knowledge, but first, I want to tell you my method. I call my method, **"SIMPLIFIED $ALES".** And if you trust me and follow you will soon think of yourself as more than an order taker, more than a customer service rep, more than an administrator. You will think of yourself as a hardheaded soft-mouthed warm sales person, representing the corporation team that wants to make PROFIT.

I am telling you that it is a " RARE PERSON WHO CAN TAKE CARE OF HEARTS WHILE ALSO TAKING CARE OF BUSINESS". (Arthur Unknown) And by the way, this is my secret, my system, my method, and my answer to making sales simple.

"Onward, Upward and Forward"
...(my own saying)

CHAPTER 4 - THE HARD HEAD SOFT MOUTH METHOD

There are six basic parts to my method:

I. Motivation/Incentive
II. Personality/Technique
III. My Sales Methods
IV. Product Knowledge
V. The Close
VI. Follow Up

First off, understand that eye-to-eye and tele-marketing are both sales. First account and cross selling are both sales. However, the words tele-phone, telemarketing and cross-selling scare peo-ple off. So change the scary feeling into a safe sale feeling and it will be your first start. After all, 85% of our first contacts with any type of business customers are by phone and if we didn't say the words telemarketing or cross selling, it wouldn't even faze us.

Not many people work on only commission so incentives have to include others things. You, the employee, must think you are lucky because you can work and not worry about how much money you've made today. The advantage is you can soft sell, be nice, not push people, smile, be kind, be considerate, talk a while and still get paid. There is nothing harder than working a whole day (8 to 5), knowing you gave your best and at the end of the day, knowing you made no money. That happens in the commission-based world. Therefore you must change your thinking from soft sales to a hard head but soft mouth sales method.

I'm sure you've thought about how much more money you can make if you were on commission. It's true no matter how hard you work when you are not on commission; your salary remains the same. But remembering no matter what you do, your salary is the security. And usually there are added benefits of insurance and 401k programs. The incentives that are in place and the extra dollars for sales that are in process here in sales give us an edge in both worlds. This should create a positive feeling.

So we (you and I) now have to come to positive realizations. I want you to think about this, because these are hard facts and how it really is and we must keep it positive....

1. If you live in a small town and not a city, often the pay is less but – it is nice to have a job.

2. If you live in a city and not a small town, the salary or commission is usually a little higher due to the cost of living and the customer base has to be larger – it is nice to have a job.

3. When you call on the phone, you listen to a variety of people, or if you have a person to person sales job you see a variety of people – it is nice to have a job

4. Tell yourself the pay is good – often better than other companies – it is nice to have a job

5. If your building is pleasant and your parking is good, – it is nice to have a job.

6. If you are self-employed – it's nice to be living in the USA where you can be a small entrepreneur – it is nice to have a job.

7. Yes, of course there are changes and growing pains, but remember there are many applicants out there that would love to have your job.

8. You should want to show management that you are the BEST and no one is better. **This is personal motivation**.

You are the one that came in and asked for the job, the business did not come looking for you. With that said, ***Go onward, upward and forward every hour, every day.***

Remember: ***"Those on top of the mountain didn't fall there."***...Richard Coniff.

Bear in mind that you either own your own business or are working for a business, - both always **GROWING AND LOOKING FOR PROFIT.** It is not the same as it used it be. I can say that because it never is. When you look back you remember the small, warm family handshake type of sales where everyone knew everyone. Businesses are now bigger and different than before. The battle of those who have been here for years and years, committed, loyal and doing things one way vs. those who are young and new and full of computer knowledge, excited about change and challenge has now bloomed. Being self-employed is even harder trying to juggle it all.

The "Mom and Pop" businesses that are so American are few and far between. The "Mom and Pop" style is the same, but today they have to have large corporation thoughts. So your thinking must CHANGE to BIND together to help each other grow, each department, each branch, each company, selling and cross selling.

This is why communication is so important. Going to community events, and chamber meetings. Helping with benefits. Having phone conferences and being sure to keep updated on what's going on in the other businesses of your type. What is the appetizer at the other restaurant? Does your competitive bank have free checking? Is the real-estate company down the street setup with a more attractive website? Compare all the different insurance rates from all companies so you can be a step ahead. In the small business world, you have to research the target market and see what the other companies are doing.

This combined with your own staff binding together for the good of the company will set you apart. It's a simple concept and actually it has always been there. It is called teamwork. If you are in management, you know that it is better to have one person working with you than three working for you. And believe me we all know it is really tough to go it alone. We all need people.

This does not mean the "handshake" method does not work, but it does mean credibility, credentials, results, experience, PROFIT must be included. It is still a personality world. It is a hard world – keeping the customer feeling special and loyal is much more difficult today. It means respect for each other, product knowledge, education and co-operation.

This puts to mind what one of my mentors once told me. "Sales is like school, you learn everything you need to know in kindergarten. That's where you learned all the basics of life. Be sure to say 'please' and 'thank you'; take your turn, and share." That's it. Same with life and the same with sales.

This combined with your own warmth, your own style; your own personal touches are the key to success in selling. **SIMPLIFIED $ALES** works for all types of employees. It's a thinking process.

However in the back of your head, no matter how simple you think this is, you must always think PROFIT. I say it again, HARD HEAD, SOFT MOUTH.

*"Many hands, hearts and minds generally contribute to anyone's notable achievement"...
Walt Disney*

I. MOTIVATION/INCENTIVE
(Positive Thinking)

The first important thing in sales is self-motivation. But before I get into the true motivation/incentive theory, I have to go backwards and show you that positive thinking has to be linked with this category. Happiness and positive thinking has to become natural, it is a part of the balance of life. Positive thinking has to be a theory of your everyday life. It is my job to reach out to you, motivate you, give you incentive to do what you have to do in life not only successfully, but also happily.

Let me go back to the basics. We have two very basic human needs:

Psychological needs and Physiological needs

Psychological Needs:

> ***Love (acceptance)***
> ***Self-esteem***
> ***Security***

And all three of these we all need to give as well as receive.

Physiological Needs:

> *Air*
> *Food*
> *Water*
> *Rest and activity, and*
> *Controlled temperature (this is a new one, seems like we can't*
> > *live without air conditioning anymore.)*

These are very basic needs, and an individual will not be motivated to meet the basic needs of his body until he becomes aware of those needs.

But we also have other needs. Some of us need others, some of us need to be alone and some need to do for others.

HOW MANY OF YOU ARE PEOPLE PLEASERS? I know I am and Why? Three reasons. One is that we don't want to be disliked; one is that we are just servants and want to be helpful and one is that it makes you feel good to contribute to someone else's life. These carry out in the sales world. Some sell just to make the boss happy, some just to make their husband happy. Put it in the back of your head, you have to sell to make PROFIT for you and the company.

It is important the customers like and trust you, but more important that you are respected so don't coat the facts. We must first please ourselves and NEVER hurt others. Keep the attitude up and be positive about how you are and what makes you tick and happy as well as the customer. Stay concise and honest and never lose your dignity.

Positive thinking in the sales world is like the friend world. If you want a friend, then need a friend. This is also a two-way street, if a friend needs you; they want a friend. Customers think you are their friend. If they need you, you better listen and that will make you feel good. It gives you a warm feeling inside of you. It's like the feeling you get when we had our babies. How good we feel holding and loving them. Why? Cause we are giving love and receiving love at the same time.

So that brings me to my question. Why, as adults, don't' we hold and hug each other? We still all hug babies, right? The answer is none of us want to be rejected...adults reject adults...babies do not reject you.

When my middle daughter was involved in "operation snowball", they had a ritual called "warm fuzzies". It was piece of yarn around the neck with little pieces hanging down. You gave a piece of the yarn to a friend and that entitled them to a hug. Any excuse being able to hug without the guilt. Too bad we can't come up with a good excuse to get hugs and even more so, too bad we need an excuse.

So if you feel good about yourself and have a positive thinking attitude, you will realize the hug is

37

just an outward expression. And since we can't go around hugging, you will have to feel the warmth inward and that will carry you through the day. But you need confidence and good feelings to let this work for you. That comes with a positive thinking attitude automatically. This can become natural. Try it.

"When friends are near, hearts abound in love."...Author Unknown

The first important thing in sales is self-motivation. (I know I said this before.) As a sales person, you must be an aggressive, clear, fast-talking, enthusiastic person. This must come though the telephone or through your eyes as you speak to a person. You must WANT the business. You have to keep that hard head PROFIT on the brain at all times. It is a personal matter and it is a personal responsibility to motivate you.

Let me help you take that responsibility in hand. Self-discipline plays an important role. In fact, it is the key. I can only tell you all of this; you are the ones that have to do it. I will continue to teach and you continue to do. OK?

1. **First, you must arrive to work on time or early.**

Get oriented, relaxed and then get right to work. Don't forget to leave your worries in the car. Everyone has problems and everyone cares a little, but really you have to keep them out of the work place, or they will fester inside you. They will only hold you back so forget them; you can gather them back up on your way home. The faster you get to work, the faster the first sale comes. The faster the first sale comes, the more motivation builds because you are ready to meet the need of that customer.

2. **We all know telemarketing and customer selling is a game of numbers.** (Back to the Las Vegas phone room)

So you must dial the phone or be ready to wait on each customer as they come in. The more customers you reach or see, the more you pitch, and the more you pitch, the more you close and the more you close the more you sell and isn't that name of the game. It is the same way with face-to-face sales, the more customers you meet, and the better you deal with them, and the better you perform, the better the service and the better the sales. Oh yes, let's not forget, also the better the PROFIT. Motivation is personal; you are responsible for your own self-discipline and your own happiness. I found the biggest downer with sales people is usually a personal problem, a sick child, or an argument with their spouse – it all affects the salesperson. Sales people by nature are very open and outgoing people, so everything shows. You can hear it on the phone or see it on their face. Again, I stress to you — keep the negative away when you are at work. Yes, it is OK to share some of the problems with your co-workers, but after five minutes, it's time to get on with work. Keep the problems to a minimal and learn to smile and enjoy your workday. It's your job. The fact remains that all emotions show and come through the phone and through your eyes.

3. There is no secret on eliminating the problems, but we can eliminate the negative of the problems with an "I Can" attitude (Zig Ziglar's motto).[1*]

Smile, be happy, and be assertive. My mom was positive. This is a habit. Complaining is habitual too, but so is smiling. I agree you have to force yourself to smile and then it will become the habit. It certainly worked in my family. My mom would not put up with anything but a smile. "Life is not that hard" she would say. Or she would say, "In the scheme of life, this is not a big problem. Deal with it, or don't deal with it – your choice, but only you can fix it". I certainly agree with her that you have to deal with it while you are at work. You have to put in your eight hours so you might as well be happy about it. Put all those "issues" out of your head and think positively —think sales. This all goes back to the hard head soft mouth method.

A back of the head attitude that you can develop is that whatever the problem is today, a month from today it won't matter anymore.

Some salespeople seem to have a more difficult time selling in the month of December because of Christmas financial worries not only for the salesperson but the customers. My secret or game still is to tell myself on December 1st, that one month from today, it will all be over. This worked for me. I could function that

---

1* Zig Ziglar, **See You at the Top**, Pelican Publishing Company, 1986

day without thinking how much I had to do for Christmas or what it was costing.

How many times have you stopped for coffee at a fast food drive-thru on your way to work and felt like you were greeted by someone who is tired or sad. If they are happy and smile, you will start out happier as well. Well, remember, sometimes you are the first contact for that customer that comes into your business.

It is your job to be up and happy, so they can be happy. Force yourself. It is contagious. You know some customers just can't handle being nice alone. Motivation is up to you. I call my morning smile a "pay forward" gift. I smile, they smile. The next person smiles and so on and so on. What a nice small gift in the am. Remember the song, "Smile and the whole world smiles with you...cry and you cry alone". Same here.

Just a little trick for you...next time you are at McDonald's and in a good mood, pay for the car's coffee behind you. It will make their day and yours too. It is also just plain fun.

So, let me say it again:

If you are late today – you'll sound hurried or look hurried. (Therefore be on time).

If you are tired – you'll sound tired and look slow and boring (Therefore, get your sleep).

If you're having a bad sales day – be careful because you can sound and look desperate. For sure then you won't make a sale. It just works that way. Because the more you sell, the more you sell. It gets inside you, in your blood, in your veins. You know what I mean, when you have a good sales day; it is usually a <u>very</u> good sales day.

Teamwork helps here. You can feed off each other, joke with each other or make nice, nice. It keeps the sanity. Competition will fall into play when one sells, then another and then another. It is like positive thinking, it is contagious.

Every day is a new day – If you didn't sell yesterday, try to forget it because today is a new day. You see, there is no way to turn back the clock, but you can wind it up again. So get on with it. Don't complain about what happened or say, "I should have, I could have, I would have". Yesterday is over. I am a firm believer that shoulda's, woulda's and coulda's will kill you.

"You have to do your own growing up, no matter how tall your father was."...Anonymous

Keep in mind that you are responsible for your part. To quote Zig Ziglar in his book, **See You at the Top***, ***"You are the only one who can use your ability. It is an awesome responsibility."*** Sales work is NOT easy. In fact, it is hard work. But I guarantee you if you keep your morale up, and keep motivated, you will make money not only for you but also for your company.

<u>Incentive</u>

I must link incentive with motivation. The difference being, motivation is your own responsibility while incentive is more the company's responsibility. This is where the company plays a role. Most of the time it (the company) is represented by a sales manager or supervisor and they have to set the incentives. If you're self-employed this is a little harder, as you have to give yourself incentive. Maybe an occasional day off. Whereas if you have a supervisor, he can be compassionate and listen to your needs, yet strict enough to keep you all working and working hard.

Coffee, occasional food, good environment, small perks, gifts, and bonuses keep the workers happy. Good manuals, communication, training, product knowledge, outlining features and benefits will definitely help the worker care and grow. Company benefits, like the health plan, 401k's, IRA'S for self employed, days off, vacation time, regular pay raises as well as a decent salary keep the personnel secure. Retaining your personnel is so important. It saves training time and doesn't waste precious hours. These are all a must.

But in spite of all this, the deal is simple. You, the employee gives them, the company, eight hours and they, the company, give you an eight-hour paycheck with or without benefits. When you don't work, you don't' get paid, and when you do work, you do get paid. That is it – that's the entire agreement and everyone is NOW happy. Nothing more is expected of each other. Of course you have to like what you are doing and want to learn and grow and the company needs to like and respect you and want you to learn and grow. Incentive is meant to be ego boosters. The company needs to listen for your needs and in turn you will listen for your customer needs. The old saying of you being the administrators customers is true. Find a happy employee and you will see them service a happy customer.

While I was working at the hard-core telemarketing job in Las Vegas, one of the incentives Mike (the boss) had was to give each of us a quarter at the beginning of the shift. We had a pac man machine (it was Vegas!!!) and since we pitched on the phone 45 minutes and off for 15-minutes. We could play pac man with our quarter, but only if we had a sale. Our aim was to have one game running the whole four hours we were on the phone. If we as a team managed this, then we got a free lunch. You can imagine how hard we worked to keep the sales up to keep the machine running so we could have a free lunch. You can call it incentive or teamwork, whatever, as long as it worked. Mike made more money, the company made more money and we made more money. And all this equals PROFIT. (That's what it's all about, right?)

Teaching and training and coaching all are necessary evils that become management's responsibility. But management can only do so much; you must cooperate because basically you are the one that counts. No one can blame management for a bad sales day. It continues to be your personal deal because you are the one doing the selling and you are the one in front of the customer.

Management and you must come to an agreement to help each other, but ultimately you still have to be the one that uses your own judgment and your own personality and technique on how to handle your customer and do your best for you, the customer and the company all at the same time. Remember, the customer first, the company first, then the sale. That's right I said both of them are first.

There are other ways the company can help. They have contests and rewards. Some give out stars. Some give out cold cash. Some give out kudos. They can send you to training classes and provide extra educational reading materials. They all work and I personally think they are all necessary. I found myself with my employees being sure to say to them "I see your work" when I saw them do something extra. That seemed to be enough to keep some going. A free lunch or a gift card is an add on. But remember everyone is working for dollars – and the deal is you get paid for the hours you work and nothing else should be expected. If more comes, then lucky you.

One more time I repeat myself. The first and most important thing in sales is the motivation. It shows you and your personality. It comes down to you vs. the person on the other end, whether phone or face-to-face. Because no matter how you say it, every time someone calls or comes in – a sale is made. Either you sell them or they sell you and I PREFER TO DO THE SELLING.

My parting remark on motivation is that you must want the sale, you must love your work, and you must love having a job. You must push yourself to be positive and you will accomplish it. This I PROMISE.

Different is different, but not wrong"...
Author Unknown

II. PERSONALITY/TECHNIQUE

The second most important thing in sales is your personality. It must show at all times. Now each of us has our own personality and we must find out what works for us.

I happen to combine my pitch with a personal touch and lots of business using my hard head soft mouth method. I am a very concise, factual seller and I believe strongly in the KISS system (Keep It Simple Stupid). I prefer to think of the acronym as Keep It Simple – Sell It.

I do try to <u>hit on something</u> that they can relate to, but then I always get right back to business. I am so fortunate:

My secret to sales is right here "taking care of the hearts while taking care of business,"

Every one of my customers was made to feel special. I spoke to them by name. If I saw them at the grocery store, I remembered them. I listened and I showed them I cared – because I did and I do! In my heart each one was special and they felt that.

However, technique and personality must be combined. We have our own personalities and we have our own techniques. Myself, I have more of a boiler room technique, which I learned to soften for bank sales. I had to work very hard at toning it down, and adding a little personality to my pitch, because I had been trained to hard sell and that was sometimes too harsh for a bank. I wanted to be warm and have them feel warmth, but never, never, never lose my professional or business-like close. And this is what I mean by **"hard head soft mouth"** – my own method.

Understand, technique is my strong point. I do not use the laid-back method. Some people do. They are soft and sweet and warm and kind. I am not that person, so if I used it I would appear fake. I can't use any laid-back method and the reason is — it doesn't work for me. Some people feel it's the only way, but my problem is with the laid-back method is I create a friend and not a sale. Sometimes it creates a call back for me and I learned a long time ago that callbacks never work. I need to make the sale today – meet their needs today. I am a strong believer that people justify their decisions in their heads and are happy if you have met their needs. However, if they have to think about it or you have to call them back, it gives them time to justify not needing the product (buyer's remorse).

So whatever works for you is OK, but you can trust by the experience I have had, that I truly believe that you must stay a little hard to increase the volume.

Hard head sales is easier via the phone than eye to eye, but try it eye to eye, you will be pleasantly surprised how it works. Again, a thinking process – that works – **YOU MUST THINK SALES**. However, think with your head and not with your mouth.

There are variations in technique; because there are variations in personality. Don't misunderstand me; you still have to be nice. Even though I sound all business, I remember children's names and ask, "how is your mother" to the right person, and am sure to smile in their eyes. I would say how nice they are, or touch an elderly's hand when their spouse has died. And the warmth in my heart is real, and the business in my mind is real too. Again, this is my secret. It is true that I really care. But I also really believed in whatever I was selling as well as in myself. I felt strongly the customer's needs and I tried hard to meet them. I can honestly say that I have always felt very good and honest and fair about my sales methods.

With all that said, you still have to do this with dignity. One of my favorite songs **THE GREATEST LOVE OF ALL**, by Whitney Houston says it exactly. No matter what, you cannot lose your dignity. There is no greater loss than that. And once you know you do have dignity, you can believe in yourself, trust yourself, and build your self-confidence. This all combined will make it easier for you to reach your sales goals.

I know that I am stressing that the hard sales method works. But I also think you have to be confident enough and strong enough to know where the responsibility lies. Some of it lies with the customer.

Teddy Behrendt

Put some of the responsibility back on the customer.

Example 1: Watch a woman in a dress shop. She sees a dress she really likes, but knows she doesn't have the money right now for it; and doesn't need it either. But she likes it and wants it. She will walk around the store avoiding the dress, but continuously circles back by it.

Leave her alone. Put the responsibility on her on how she is going to handle this. If the clerk haunts her, she'll be distracted and will not be able to think how she is going to pay for it. The sale will be lost. But give her space. She is thinking "pretty dress". She is thinking maybe if she tries it on it won't fit. But it does. She is thinking maybe she can charge it and pay next month when there is more money coming in. She is just thinking and thinking until she works it out in her head how she can do this. She is also justifying that she can wear it next week to a graduation party. That would make it OK. Once the struggle is over in her mind, she will make the decision. You cannot help her. But once she decides how this will work out, she has also decided that the dress is hers. The sale is made. She sold herself. It was her decision. You just need to smile and give a little nod of approval and go for the close. After the sale, she will be happy with her decision because she took this responsibility on herself.

Example 2: The Vice President of the Bank where I worked was dealing with a large commercial loan customer. He had wined and dined the customer several times and asked me to come along as a retail expert if the customer had any questions. The customer was concerned about how we would handle some things versus another bank he was also looking at. I presented all the facts on how we could service him. Still over a month went by and he couldn't decide. He called me and asked if we could go again to lunch to discuss some detailed questions. I simply explained to him that I felt that we had discussed as much as we could. I had no more benefits to offer that we hadn't discussed except that with our bank, he would also get me, and I would work really hard for him. I said very nicely, "Let me know when you have made a decision. I can't do that for you." (hard head). " And, thanks so much for your consideration of our bank and thank you especially for calling me." (soft mouth). THE END. I put the decision right in his lap. The vice president was just a little upset with me, but I told him. "You keep throwing the ball to him to make a touchdown and he keeps throwing it back to you and you keep catching it. Eventually one of you has to go for the goal. Well, now the ball is in his court." The next day the customer called the vice president and said, "SOLD. Sorry it took me so long but I needed help in making the decision. But I know I made the right choice now. Teddy helped make the decision for me."

Sometimes you have to give a little nudge to help the customer to quite procrastinating. But be careful to read them correctly, because this could have completely backfired on me. And that would have been sad. I would have lost a large long-term commercial customer. It isn't easy to be a little hard on the customer, but there were times, at least in my career, that it became a part of my technique.

"It's our faults that make us human."... Author unknown.

My personal technique is:

Always be loud

(I don't mean yell, but project to be heard and clear) – It does so many things. It causes enthusiasm, creates energy throughout the room, gets your adrenaline running and most of all, the buyer can hear you.

Be completely in control of the conversation at all times

Acknowledge the person as they speak to you about their personal situations, respond, support them, but lead them back to business as tactfully and quickly as possible.

Always, always get the first name

By using the first name or sir, or mam (madam) – it keeps the attention level up. When you say their name and they are writing, they will stop and look up. You can do the same thing eye to eye when they start leafing through a catalog, it will refocus them. Just say their name, it puts it all back in control.

Never ask a question that can be answered with the word, NO

Never say, "Is that right?"   Say, "Right?
Never say, "Is that fair enough?"   Always say, "fair enough?"

Never rush a customer on the phone or at the counter.

A smile goes a long way.

Do not anticipate the objective

If you start eliminating all objectives before they give you one, you leave yourself no room to rebut or explain.   When they ask a question, you then give your best factual answer. This is what is called answering the objective. And, after each objective is answered, you can close again. But if you've already eliminated the objective, you lost the sale yourself.

The first one to speak loses

This is a very basic rule that works. If you present a rebuttal or ask a closing question and there is a silence in the conversation. Wait it out, because the first one to speak after a lull loses. (You can test this at home when you argue with your mate or your child. You'll see this works in all walks of life.) This is a very effective rule.... one you need to remember and use. **IT WORKS. WRITE IT DOWN.**

Be sure to thank them

And always ask if there are any questions. Be sure that they understand the terms. Then you can go to the next item when you are clear with the first. This builds trust. Then, after the close, genuinely, in their eyes, say "thank you".

As I said earlier, there are reasons why you must vary your technique and personality. You have to alter your pitch by sexes: I need to say that I completely think men and women are equal and I favor neither, but I did a year's worth of surveys studying the different pitch methods by the different sexes and the following are my personal results.

1. **<u>Woman to woman</u>** – Women sell well to other women especially if they are both tough. They love control. And buying or selling is control. You can put it on them to make a decision. Women thrive on decision-making. Be aware, if it is the woman that makes the appointment it is the woman that will make the decision.

2. **<u>Woman to man</u>**– You can joke with a man when you're a woman. Absolutely never get risqué but a little fun goes a long way with a man. He can hear your smile, men love women that smile. Always treat a man with respect on all the issues. My personal survey proved that respect is the #1 need for a man. Be aware if the man makes the appointment, it will be the man who makes the decision.

3. **<u>Man to woman</u>** – He can use his wiles, but much more carefully, because women get angry if they think he's flirting. Man to woman should stay business-like. Respect her, let her make the decision – she feels she conquered him. That works – try it. After all a sale is a sale especially when it comes from the heart.

4. **<u>Man to man</u>** – The hardest of all. Men's conversations have a way of being more "BS" than sales. They play games more than women do. Women are tough nuts – men pretend more. Men have a hard time agreeing. It can become a difficult situation. They will go off on

tangents about sports, politics, cars, etc. and create a friend rather than a sale. Men tend not to follow the pitch as written, they make up their own. This sometimes causes problems with the close. Some men think they know better what to say than what's written, but once you convince them to follow the pitch and it works and they sell, you will sell a huge increase in PROFIT.

This is just fun.... maybe not needed in your line of business, but it goes along with the personality flavor. Think about it- use it a little – not to an extreme – but I promise it will help.

As I told you earlier I kept a chart and tracked how we all worked. (By the way thus was the start of this book).

This is a hard sale technique that I have compared to the soft sale. Now you must figure out your own way. Remember you CAN combine the techniques also. In fact, you better.

Whatever works for you? Do a little hard sales, do a little soft sales (but always keep the hard head soft mouth method in your mind), add to that your personality, keep it to business, but be sure to add pleasure – mix it up, figure it out – find your style, your own system – your own technique. But somehow just do it and you will see results.

"Believe in Everybody, Depend on Nobody"...Author Unknown

III. MY SALES METHODS

The reason I compare hard sales to soft sales is because you need hard sale knowledge in your mind, with a soft sale approach. This is called "retroactive" selling. Concentrating on the customer and not the sale. This method works best for financial institutions compared to hard sale or "proactive selling" used by car salesmen.

History shows that financial institutions have changed a great deal in the past twenty years. Remember bankers used to be order takers. Today, bankers are expected to be salespersons. Hard selling concentrates on the close rather than the product. I prefer to have you concentrate on the customer and a cross-sale. Concentrate more on selling the customer's need, rather than the bank as an institution or just one product per se. The customer will help make the close himself after you listen to them, question them and find their need. Then you close.

The six parts of the sales process are:

    A. Pre-Sales Planning (Goal Setting)
    B. Introduction
    C. The "Needs" Conversation
    D. Call to Action
    E. Follow Up
    F. The "Needs" Fulfillment (The Sale)

"It's always a good idea to plan ahead. Remember it wasn't raining when Noah built the ark"... Quote I found when reading daily inspirations by Expect Success.

A. Pre-Sales Planning

We begin by using our new sales thinking process, but there is more. We will add self-confidence, self-esteem and self-discipline to incentive/motivation, positive thinking and personality /technique in order to make it all work. And still keeping in mind, the backgrounds of our industry, where it came from and where it is going.

Along with pre-sales planning and preparation is goal setting. I have a system to goal setting and a small secret that works for me. It all starts with having a dream. You take a dream, research and check the resources and put the idea or dream into action. But at this point, usually you get bored or stuck and then the normal action is to quit on the dream and often blame others. "It's not my fault, the post office didn't deliver my letter", etc. This kills the dream. So somewhere between putting your idea into action and getting bored, you need to re-dream or redesign your dream and start over with more research and resources and new action. You will continue to get bored and blame others, but you also continue to re-dream. This is how it gets done. If you do not re-dream, you will funnel down and your dream will die.

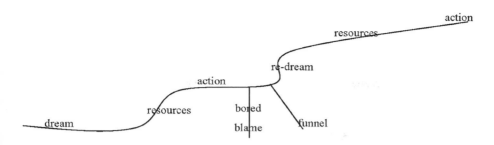

Goal setting and seeing your dream and putting it into action is preparation for all PROFIT organizations to make money as well as small businesses. It is part of the thinking in the back of the head, the preparation process.

"Good things happen when planned, bad things happen on their own"...Quality is Free

We have to add the fact that the first sale and the cross sale go hand in hand. But all this happens with action. It begins before the customer arrives. It also begins with preparation and training of your particular company's procedures and products.

Preparation includes: 1. <u>Reading brochures.</u> – If you are a car salesman, you better know each car's brochures and their features because the customer does and knows the difference. Remember that the features are the facts and benefits are the bonuses. In the banking world the feature of a checking account is the free checks – the benefit is that it makes life easier when you can write as many checks as you need without the worry of paying for them. In the insurance world, the features are the coverages of your plan and the benefits are the security you get from this policy. In the advertising world the actual pen is the feature and the advertising on the pen that spreads your name is the bonus or benefit. In the restaurant world, the feature is the menu; the benefit is the good taste of the food.

Preparation includes: 2. <u>Cheat sheets</u> – Read, outline and then prepare a cheat sheet for you that makes sense and makes your life easier to explain any details that might need explained. If you have five different types of investments, cheat sheet the advantage of each of one. If these include extras (like interest rates) be sure you know the rate sheets or the prices of each item either together or combined. If there is a break point, be sure you have that listed for the customer's benefit. Knowing the product is only half the battle, presenting it accurately is the other half. This causes integrity and quality as well as trust and achievement.

Preparation includes: 3. <u>Knowing all the advertisements</u> – and what has been put out there for the customer to see, because they seem to find things that we "the expert" never heard of. Sometimes I am sure the employee is the last to know if there is a sale or a special promotion. Following each promotion is a must. Know your competition. You will be one step ahead.

Preparation includes: 4. <u>Knowing the computer procedures</u> – If you fumble thru the computer once you have the customer's approval, they will question your credibility all over again. They will lose confidence in your skills and wonder if you knew what you were talking about when you were speaking to them. This can be a problem and can create a "RED FLAG". Be sure you know how to work the computer, the calculator and the applications ahead of time, because in the world of technology today, the computer "CANNOT" be an event, it has to be the

"NORM". And believe me this is not an easy feat in front of the customer. You have to be that special rare person who can ask questions, complete the information on the computer, keep your personality, hold a conversation, smile, deal with their hearts and sell all at the same time. A secret that will help you here and will eliminate a lot of confusion is to have the application filled out as much as possible before the customer arrives. If it is ready for signature, they will see you were prepared and knowledgeable.

"If you haven't got time to do it right, when will you have the time to do it over."?...Jeffery J. Meyer

Preparation is not just product training; it is discussion training as well. You need to know the product, you should be able to discuss the product and hold a normal conversation with the customer as you are doing all of this. You have to be so well versed in your head. It is like playing football, so well rehearsed that it just happens when the time arises. The words just flow out of your mouth to meet the need without a lot of thought process during the conversation. So again, I promote practice, preparation, common sense and a clear head. And it will all happen and happen well.

Preparation and training go hand in hand.

I'm not quite sure when one ends and one begins. They are one and the same, but different. Training is learning the facts and preparation is using the facts. Preparation and training are the beginning of the sale. There are few other things that also need to be considered like x-dating (the preparation of notes on your clients and referrals in your journal for the next several weeks). It helps to write personal notes that you might need later when you call them back or see them at a follow-up appointment. Depending on your type of business, insurance, cars, financial institutions, restaurants, you might need to record birth dates and children's names, etc. – for future references. Be sure to have a system so you will be able to find those types of facts easily when the customer leaves. Do you really think that I remembered all this off the top of my head? I kept great notes. Then it was easier to have heart. Putting birthdays on a calendar and sending cards is a very nice touch as well. Seems hokey, but people like to be remembered especially on THEIR birthday.

Practicing how to probe questions. Remembering not to ask a question that can be answered with the word "no. Practicing with yourself in your head over and over again is good preparation and training. Role-playing is used a lot for preparation, but most sales people do not like role-playing, as it can't really imitate the actual scenario, so I advocate practicing out loud. Practice in front of a mirror and practice in your head. You know that anything can change throughout the conversation and you know you have to adapt to the change of thinking or the change of heart at any time in the conversation. This is so important and needs to be instinctive. It has to become a natural process.

I have one more thought that can help you with preparation and that is to set your priorities early in life. Think about the order of life or the circle of life. It is part of the whole picture. This circle gives you a way to see more than the outside of the customer. It gives you a look at their insides as well.

In the center is YOU (I call it SELF). The next outer circle is family, and then church, then occupation and the last circle being community.

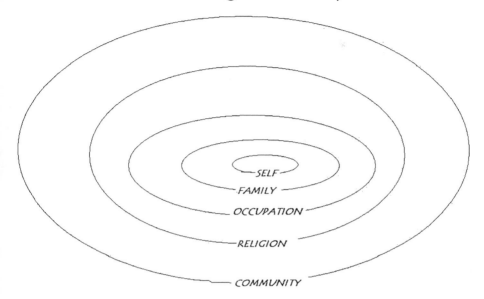

This is just an order of life, but sometimes, people get into a circle to an extreme. Some business people get stuck doing everything for nothing in the community and their family and occupation are then hurting. This has a tunnel effect and you spiral downward. Some are too much into their family and it hurts the community or corporation or their own business. And some are into religion that runs over into the other parts of their life. All these circles are important, but they have to be done in balance. This helps in preparation and goal setting. If you listen carefully to the customer, and think about the circles, sometimes, you will be able to hear the need easier. You yourself have to be balanced as well and you have to be able to see if your customer is in balance or if they are leaning to one circle more than another. If you know this, you can speak and work with them more intelligently. It keeps life in prospective. But many of us go to extremes with one of the five circles. Listening and getting to know your customers is very helpful in order to sell the proper need. They too are often stuck in one circle.

Every customer and every situation is a little different, so no one can teach you how to handle all situations, but you need to be as prepared as much as you can for whatever type of person, conversation or reaction occurs. This will help you be more of an expert. Outsiders see you in a suit and they automatically think you are an expert, so you better act like one.

And then, when you have all this learned training down pat, your salesmanship will enter the picture. Again Incentive Motivation and Personality Technique are all a part of this; as well as your appearance. There has to be a holistic approach – that means you will be using your mind, body and spirit to make up your day.

Mind, Body and Spirit

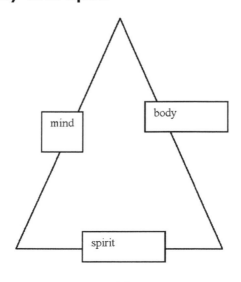

B. Introduction

Interpersonal communication is communication with each other. This can be done in three ways:

Body language,
Voice Tone, and
Words;

And verbal communication or words is, at times, the least important.

I use some basic rules to help make this beginning communication a little easier and start it right.

1. The salesperson should be the one to start the communication. This is called "active communicator". The good thing about this is that it allows the customer to react to your personality and technique rather than you to his.

2. When any customer enters your office, you should stand

Ask if you can shake their hand and begin the conversation. (Some companies are insisting that you ask to shake hands due to the privacy act.)

Example:
Good Afternoon, my name is ____
This is the holistic approach I mentioned earlier:

Mind –"Start conversation"
Body – "Stand"
Spirit – "Extent Hand"

ALL OF THIS WITH A SMILE — creates a warmth and security. It is nice to offer them a coffee or a soda, and when they sit down, you know they are there for a while. Treat them like they have come into your home.

Quite simple and very affective == everyone tells you this, but few do it   WHY??????

3. **You, as the seller, want control of the conversation**.

Transactional Analysis developed by Eric Berne (1950's)* was the first significant theory of interpersonal communication. Berne identified three personality styles a child, parent and adult.

Childlike Behavior – Sometimes results come from being childlike, which I define as the salesperson "getting what he wants." Don't whine, speak.

Parent like Behavior – This is the behavior that sparks change. It's an attitude and attitudes are contagious. Make sure yours is worth catching. If it's not good, it can cause a reaction rather than a response, so you have to use this carefully. Don't give orders, but sound confident– credible.

Adult Behavior – This comes across using all the previous aspects: our dress, our sitting methods, and professional questions. Don't Lord over the customer, but be the one that knows and teaches and helps.

---

* <u>Games People Play, Eric Berne,</u> revised copyright 1964, Grove Press

All three behaviors, if not used to extreme, work and can be worked together. This is the transactional analysis. It is the first significant theory of interpersonal communication. This simply means that all people use all three transactions to communicate. Everyone understands this language, so we need to be aware of the focus as seller or sellee, because the sellee often uses this same method on you and then they become the seller.

When we communicate we do so in distinct ways. We use the following to help us:

Space
Pitch
Words
Touch
Body Language

I mentioned this at the beginning of this chapter, but to elaborate won't hurt.

Space – This is an interesting concept. Automatically, formal people require more than informal people. Give it to them. Let them breathe. Read them correctly – they are not withdrawing so much as just being very cautious. More casual open people will lean into you when they speak. They are not as reserved, but they are not any easier to sell. They will not require as much space as formal people. They are just more relaxed.

Pitch – We need to project and be concise. Speak up so that you can be heard. We tend to drop the end of our sentences and then the customers tries to assume what you said. They usually will not ask you to repeat yourself. Assuming is not a good thing, sometimes they hear you incorrectly and that can cause a miscommunication. Some customers (usually the more formal type) will speak with a loud pitch – they are part of the parent like behavior (transactional analysis) and this tends to cause a childlike behavior in return. You must be the one that is clear or the roles will reverse and the customer will then become in control.

Words – Always remain professional. Do not speak over the customer's heads. Use descriptive words, factual words, not flowery words or vague words. Be more precise than cute – do not use words like "cool" or "sweet". Slang is annoying. Profanity is out of the question. It is never in good taste. Traditional words are a common language and everyone understands them. In some professions, (like banking) you need to be careful about abbreviations. Example: everyone doesn't know that APY is annual percentage yield. So go beyond and spell it all out clearly. Even if you feel you have said the same words a hundred times, continue to have a pattern and a style that is yours and clear and simple. **KISS – "Keep it Simple Stupid"**. Comparing basic words to big words helps. Example: in the restaurant business "our five-meat buffet" says it better than "our extravaganza buffet", even if it doesn't sound as eloquent. No matter how you say it, the customer is still going to ask what is on the buffet?

Touch – Let's talk about touch. We must be very careful with this. Our society confuses physical touch with "getting too close". But a pat on the hand if they seem confused draws their attention back to your words. Remember when you introduced yourself, you stood and shook their hands.

That breaks the barrier from the beginning and re-moves a lot of the uncomfortable fears. And even though I continue to tell you to stand and shake their hands, it is still a rare approach among sales-people to do so. Again, why? Let me clarify ex-actly what a handshake does: A handshake is an assertive statement. Formal business people like to handshake to begin the interaction. An informal, shyer person likes to handshake because it breaks the barrier. Men like to handshake: makes them feel in control: women like to handshake; makes them feel equal. So, why don't we do this? Do we just forget? Are we too shy? Or are we just lazy? But remember to ask if you can touch them or if you can shake their hand, it is a new ruling. Ex: "May I shake your hand, I am so happy you are here."

Body Language – We all know about body lan-guage. It's how we sit in the chair, how we stand. A couple of months ago, I was asked to help train an investment salesperson. She knew her product very well, but could not make a sale. While observ-ing her, it finally dawned on me that her body ap-peared closed up as she sat at her desk. It looked like she didn't know what she was talking about. She was quite tall and unconsciously trying to hide her tallness. The connotation was that she had no confidence in her self. She would speak cor-rectly but when she sat at her desk, she slumped over. It made her look like she was tired and sad and not very smart. None of that was true, but her stance gave you that feeling. I finally said to her. Do you think if you put your shoulders back and head up just a little, not too much that you look like a snob, that you might give the customer a bet-ter feeling. I think you make me feel like you are not sure of what you are talking about because you are slumping and your head is down. She looked at me and said, "Well, I am tall and I feel big and ugly when I sit tall". "No way" I said. "You need to be the best you can be. And slumping doesn't get it." She smiled and sat up and looked up a little. She continued to pitch me. I could hear her better, she was clearer, I could see her smile and her eyes looked full of knowledge. I do think that was her biggest draw back. The customer was uncomfortable with her body language (although they didn't know that was it). Talking with her this past month, I learned she has made her first investment sale. She says she feels a lot more comfortable. She has decided to stand tall as well, not braggy tall, just natural tall. She said I have slumped forever and it does make you tired. She said her attitude had completely changed and now she feels better about herself. I know it is only one small thing but sometimes that is all it takes, one small thing, to help make the sale and the sale is PROFIT.

Just a few more things about body language. Try to follow the customer's lead, ask them to sit, and then you sit. If they stand, you stand. When the deal is completed, stand again and ask to shake hands again. Be sure to thank them for the business. A little nod is often appropriate. It says so much. A smile says more. Be grateful to them and feel like you met their need. Feel in your head (hard sales) that you are there for them to do MORE business later. Be sure they think you are their friend (soft sales), and be sure to remember to say something personal and kind to them. Example: (if they are going away next week) ..."have a nice vacation" or "Your business is very important and thank you for choosing me."

This is not easy to explain because you have to respond properly with the proper move and gesture that the customer leads you through. However, even though you have your own style, you must understand this is very important. This needs to be genuine, "for real". Some of this is a learned behavior; it is not all natural although hopefully some of it comes naturally since you are a nice person. Again, this is my secret – caring – really caring, "for real",

"Effective interpersonal communication requires you to make spot judgments about the person whom you are communicating with, and to know how you appear in the eyes of your customer. It takes two people. Effective communication leads to effective selling. If you don't quickly size up your customer, then you will be in an to order-taking mode."   (Cross-Selling Financial Services), page 102 Dwight S. Ritter.[2*] These distinct characteristics can result in customer change if used properly.

So don't assume or prejudge as you meet the customer about their personality or their financial status. You can make an adaptation to someone else's personality as you listen and observe them.

Along with this, you have to think about the tone of your voice. Nice words do not sound nice if you have a hard tone. Be careful. "Ninety percent of the friction of daily life is caused by the wrong tone of voice."…Life's Little Instruction Book for Couples.[3*]

---

2 * **Cross Selling Financial Services**, Dwight Ritter, John Wiley and Sons, 1988

3 * **Life's Little Instruction Book for Couples**, H. Jackson Brown, Rutledge Hill Press, 2000

C. The "Needs" Conversation

I have been thinking about this part for a long time. The need of the customer has to be met and how do we go about that intelligently. It comes naturally to some of us, but most of us have been trained order takers, so it is not so natural. Listening for the need is the whole idea, but how does that come about without sounding nosy, or sounding like a sergeant, or sounding like you just want a sale. I know you have been told it is all conversation and that is correct, but there must be a method to your conversation. I hope to help you in this area. This is a very important process and it should not be taken lightly. To me it is the core of the sales — It is the tree trunk. Conversation, product, computer knowledge, probing, eye contact, body language, are the branches.

They help make the trunk stronger and the tree more attractive. The tree being the product. This is the section that creates the attitudes of "I'm not a salesman". Or "I hate sales." Or, "Just let me do my job, I know what I'm doing". Or "I can't really sell anything to anyone". And so, this is exactly the reason for my book on "Simplified Sale".

I want to teach you how to ask questions without feeling like you are selling the world to the customer. I want to teach you that conversation is selling. And that conversation is more than a personal conversation. It is a planned conversation that you have in your head. And all the while you are THINKING sales._

My theory of hard head soft mouth really applies here.

You must have a kind heart.

You need to use mind body and spirit together to create a kind heart, and yet be you at the same time; as well as WANTING to sell. You continue to think of the customer and the company and of the PROFIT. But you always know that the customer comes first.

The customer is your main focal point.

You do not want to talk them into something that does not meet their need. It is not right, it is not fair and it is not what they want. Unfortunately, however, they don't always know what they want. So it is your job to find out exactly what they need and want and then go for it. That's hard sales with a soft mouth.

So here is one more rule:

ASK QUESTIONS THAT
PEOPLE WANT TO ANSWER

Stop and think about that. If you ask a person a question about their child, they will want to answer and they do and sometimes go on and on about their precious ones. If you ask a businessman about his business, he will talk forever about it. If you ask a football player about a certain game, they have all the answers for you. Ask your dad about his job and listen to him as he tells you what he did today or your Mom about her garden club. **People like to talk about themselves.** We all do. We don't necessarily want to brag or start the conversation, but if you ask.... well then that gives them liberty. (Be sure to take a few notes, like if a mom tells you that her child will be 2 in two weeks – the next time you see her, you can ask how the birthday went, etc.

You get the idea – (my secret). I try to remember names, relate something to the name and write that down as well, so my next conversation can be more personal.

Then it is your job to lead the personal conversation into the sales conversation so the customers are comfortable. Sadly, however, we all start to push the product much too soon or too late. We need to find out what their need is before we decide on the product for them. This is a very careful procedure. We often stay on the personal conversation too long. Soon we have made a friend and not a sale. But there is nothing wrong with making a friend <u>with</u> the sale. If they think you are their friend, and you better not be fake about this, you will get a lot more sales and referrals. Use the sandwich method, say something about the product, something personal, and then back to the product. This will build trust and confidence as well as the friendship. There is knack to this, but as you work with this thought, it becomes automatic. It is a change in sales thinking from order taking to conversational sales. I call it **SIMPLIFIED $ALES**.

D. Call to Action

I want to give you an example to stress my point and since I just retired from 22 years of banking and banking sales, I will use bank products as my example. However, this applies to all situations no matter the product.

My example is to show you that if you present the product too soon this is what you end up with.

Customer comes to office – Stand, ask to shake hands, introduce self and ask them to please sit – smiling the whole time. You say, "May I help you?" Offer coffee or soda. Customer: "Yes, I just need a checking account.

You: Certainly. Let me explain them to you — We have 3 types of accounts, the first one is our basic account. Our second one is if you only want an account for a few checks and it is called "economy" and our third one is our interest bearing account that requires a balance. Here is a brochure to help you decide.

Which seems to be the one you want?

STOP

The customer is now very uncomfortable and answers anyway he can remember. He heard certain words only; "basic", "economy", "balance". In the meantime he starts looking at the brochure in front of him, quickly trying to figure out his own needs. Sometimes at this point the customer will say – "Which do you think is the best?" You, of course, wanting a sale will pick one. OK, SOLD. So what have you done? Maybe you sold a regular account to a customer that really needed an interest bearing.   You left no room for cross selling like a debit card or online banking. You were an order taker. But the customer is OK with that and you did sell him one product – a checking account. That is not what I am talking about. That is definitely just doing a job. This was taking an order. That is not what I call being a good salesperson. You did not take care of the customer you just gave them a checking account.

So how do we do this?

We must slow down and not rush the process. During the conversational process you need to do three things at once in your mind. Ask the question, listen to the answer to find the need, and plan for your next question. Having questions in your head on each product is good preparation. It doesn't always apply, but the thinking process is helpful in each situation. Being a good listener and being a good question asker is being a good salesperson. You must truly be interested not only in your customer as a person, but what they need and why they came to you. In most sales books, they call this "probing", I prefer the word "listening". Be careful to hear every answer so you don't miss the need. You have to listen carefully in order to know the difference between the "chatter", the "intellect" and the customers "emotions".

Then you sort out the intellect to narrow down to another level with another question. It's ok to ask direct questions to see if you found the need. Then filter, in your head, so you can read the customer correctly – sometimes they aren't sure what they need, so you have to figure it out for them.

Staying with the banking business (since that's what I just came from) let's try a better example:

Customer comes to office – Stand, ask to shake hands, introduce self and ask them to please sit – smiling the whole time. You say, "May I help you? May I get you a coffee or soda?"

Customer: "Yes, I just need a checking account."

You: Great I will be glad to help you. Will you have a direct deposit into the account?

Customer: Oh no — I already have an expense checking account – I work at Wal-Mart and they direct deposit into my other bank. Why? Do you have an account more suitable for my needs?

You: Well, I think so. We do have a special account if you have direct deposit that receives interest and has many perks — the debit card is free with no fee charge for cash withdrawal from our bank at any ATM machine. You could use this one as your expense checking.

Customer: Yes but today I just want another checking account.

You: Since you already have an expense checking account, what will you be using this second account for? Or do you plan on two expense accounts?

Customer: I plan to use this as a vacation account. I like to keep my vacation money separate, I like to keep my taxes money separate and I like to keep my real estate taxes money separate.

You: I know what you mean. I'm like that too. In fact I have my home insurance and my real estate taxes as part of my house payment here. It is one less worry for me when that time rolls around.

I think you are a very good planner. Do you have a Christmas club as well? I love mine.

Customer: No – but I have definitely been wanting to do that as well. I will do that today since I am here. Been meaning to do that all year. Here it is March and I never got to it. At Christmas I will be quite upset. My two children are used to getting lots for Christmas. Every year I threaten to cut back. But I am working and product buyers do pretty well at Wal-Mart, so I plan on giving them the best Christmas I can.

You: How old are your children?

Customer: They are now 11 and 14. The boy John will be 15 in April and Jenny is 11 going on 21 – you know how girls are. My wife Kathy home schools them and they are doing very well. I am very proud of them.

You: I would be too. That is great. I will be sure we get that Christmas club started today. But you still need that second checking account to save for extras like vacations. Are you going to keep a larger balance in it? I'm thinking that if you keep a $1000 minimum we have a money market account that earns more interest than a savings. If you feel you can only keep $100 in it and have to build, I'm thinking you might want a savings in place of a checking.

Customer: No, I want a checking because I **need** that debit card. I might **need** some of the money and I don't want to be trapped, yet I don't want it to be too easy for me to spend the money either or I'll never get on a vacation.

You: I understand completely. So let's take care of it. We can open you a checking account as well as a savings. Give you a debit card where you can transfer the money from one account to another and if you decide to move your direct deposit (put responsibility on him) than you will receive interest and free benefits on loans and ATM transactions. With this automatically comes online banking. You can pay your bills on line – save time and money (feature and benefit) - and if you have a little extra just transfer automatically to your savings each month. That's what I do; it mounts up faster than you can believe. (Relate to customer). Of course you will still have your debit card for purchases, etc. I can change your direct deposit right here for you. And we can also decide on an amount for the Christmas club that can come out automatically each month.

Customer: Sounds good except that I have my electric bill already coming out of my other account. Can you change that for me too?

You: Yes, sir. I am here to help you. This is what I do best, so let me ask you, "How much money are we starting with?" (Close the sale)

LET ME STOP HERE. I could go on but we haven't covered Product or Close. I'm sure role-playing is not one of your favorite things anyway. (Remember that is the biggest complaint I get when training —" please no role-playing"). I know that it is hard to make up any scenario. We all do a much better job when we are doing it with the customer in our own office, or on their turf if you go there. I know that is true. But I hope this gives you a little insight as to how you can have a conversation and get more info than just an order.

E. The Follow Up

Looking back just briefly at the above customer. I want you to note that you uncovered many opportunities with this customer. He is a steady worker, probably has a 401K, and probably has a savings somewhere. Apparently owns a home (we might have lower mortgage rates). He has two children that need to go to college (after all, they are being home schooled and he is proud of them) so college doesn't look like an option; it looks like a "have to" in his eyes. He probably has a savings account at the other bank as well, but we have college funds. And as soon as possible we should discover the other bank and see why he came here instead of there for the 2nd checking. Once we know that – we are in deep with this customer. Already in the back of my head I am thinking, "life insurance – two children – they NEED it" I found the needs; I just need to sell them.

There is a great opportunity to continue when you meet with his wife to have the signature cards signed, etc. More conversation with both of them and more cross selling can be accomplished.

I know this was all bank related – but this kind of conversation is what works with all types of sales. Uncovering the need first – listening to the customer – not probing but encouraging to get to know his personality and let yours be known as well. Make an attempt to listen and find out what they are really looking for. They came to you (or you went to them and they allowed you in their office); so the customer is interested.

I hate to call this selling – I think of it more as a natural way to help people. I am convinced that someone is being sold something everyday –I am also convinced if a customer wants something and you don't find out what it is and give it to him, someone else will. Remember I learned that with make-up a long time ago. I just want the customer to be happy. It is a simple process – Question to question to get a proper commitment. I like to call it a <u>needs fulfillment</u>. This leads right into my next section of completing the needs fulfillment with the proper product for the customer. Too many sales people sell the wrong product.

F. Needs Fulfillment

Example: "I want to buy a home with 3 bedrooms Mr. Real Estate Agent."

Agent: "No problem, let's look at this one – it has 2 bedrooms with the possibility of the basement being turned into a 3rd bedroom, but it has a 2 car garage and that is one of your priorities."

Or: "I am looking for a 4-door car, but I am a sport car lover by heart. Having two children has destroyed my impractical nature."

Car Salesman: "I know you said that 4 doors are important, but I just want to show you this cherry red Mustang. It's a honey — then we can go further if you wish."

This is annoying to say the least and if the customer is just a bit hairyed or a bit undisciplined, they can get themselves into a situation that they will not be happy with later, wondering how it all happened. It's an art to crash and sell just like it is an art to simplify a sale — I'm not against getting the sale. I invented "Hard Head Soft Mouth". I want the money and I want PROFIT, but I want a happy customer first. I truly believe that I will retain customers and get more referrals than anyone else, if I make them happy the first time round. I believe this is ***taking care of hearts while taking care of business.***"

So listen for the need, hear the need, fill the need and make the sale properly. You will have a happy and repeating customer.

When it comes to your product or project, people will take quality as seriously as you do – no more so." Philip B. Crosby

IV. PRODUCT KNOWLEDGE

Product knowledge is important no matter the product. You must understand what you are selling. But it is the same in every situation. If you are selling cars, you better read every brochure and know every detail about each type of car you have on the lot, because your customer has already done his homework. You have to be as smart as the customer. If you are in the financial world, you better know every product in the company. At least have an idea of what it is that you are listening for so you can find and hear the need of the customer. Know the interest rates, the competitive rates, and the name of your competition's product that is comparable. Know the features and benefits of each product within the corporation. If you are selling McDonald's fast food, you better know what comes with each # and be sure to ask about what to drink and if they want dessert.

If you are self-employed, make it your business to know your competition. What they are selling the same products for, what price they are asking compared to yours. Check their style. Many customers will take a more expensive product if they like you. Do a fair comparison, because your customers will.

The special touch of personality and warmth goes a long way when you present a product. When I seat customers in the restaurant, I say, "Welcome, Have you been here before?" If they say "no", then I say, "Great, you are in for a treat." (mind set). If they say "yes", then I say, "Good, then you know how good our food is. We have the best chef." (again mind set).

In the restaurant business, you best know the specials and what makes up the specials, what kind of sauce or flavoring. Do not, however, offer too much information. You wait until the customer asks unless you can hear in their questioning a need to offer the information. Sometimes the customer at a restaurant will ask what you think is the best product. You best know — I absolutely have a hard time with a waiter or waitress that says, "it's all good" or "I don't know I haven't tried the special yet". You had better have tried it — An answer is best with another question. Example: "Are you a meat eater, or would you prefer seafood?" This narrows down the choices for your best answer and to meet their need or desire, as you would call it in the restaurant world. We sure don't want an unhappy customer in a restaurant. They tell everyone. Actually they tell with their feet. They just never come back. And that is not profitable at all. If the customer says they are a meat eater. You can say, "We sell a lot of prime rib here and the customers seem happy with that choice. Myself that is one of my favorites, but I am a meat eater as well." This is a believable answer. Rather than "its all good."

As you gathered, I work part-time in a restaurant. I love the food service work. I am convinced being a waitress goes hand-in-hand with sales.

I was asked to speak on sales at a workshop this past month on product sales. The name of my session was "The Buffet Style of Selling." I presented how restaurant sales and bank sales are not the same, but should be. I displayed the bank products on tables displayed like a food buffet and how appealing it can be to the customer just like a restaurant does with food. Banks usually just put out brochures in a heap. No one really looks at them that way. You see it is not just one showing product as much as knowing and understanding and the presentation of all the products. I have presented this particular speech two times now and I am pleased at the increased sales results in both worlds.

I also just finished doing a phone survey of all local restaurants regarding the specials and prices and the wedding plans. I put the information into a cheat sheet style and informed all the staff for "back of the head" knowledge. It has been a big asset. Its amazing what a little knowledge can do – gives confidence if nothing else. All employees do better if they believe in their own product.

I have been fortunate to help train the wait staff at this particular restaurant and PROFIT has increased. One of the reasons is that I encouraged the staff to offer a bottle of wine. If two are drinking wine; it is more reasonable to order a bottle rather than get refills. You can have 4 glasses from a bottle for the price of 3 regular glasses. (This method has increased the bottle of wine sales more than double). The reason this is so profitable is because the customers were originally only planning on having one glass of wine.

Also, we have a dessert tray that MUST be shown, even if the customers at the table say "no dessert". You still show the tray (you can say – let me show you what we do have, maybe next time you'll want to save room for one). When you bring the tray, you might even suggest they share one to try it. Usually they end up with at least one dessert if not 2 or 3. I learned that if one person says OK and orders one dessert the rest at that table will also order, because they didn't want to be the only one eating dessert. You see, restaurant customers are afraid of looking like a "pig". But you better know exactly what the desserts are and what is in them. Telling them about each one is what actually causes the sale. It increases the appetite in their mind. And cross selling is where the profit lies. So by using the dessert tray and explaining the product, PROFIT has increased again. Desserts and sodas have the largest profit margin, except for bar items (of course). So another means of sales that has worked in this business, is to say when they sit down. "May I get you something from the bar? Our special tonight is strawberry margaritas, regular or virgin if you so desire." If they were just going to have water or a soda product, this will often help them decide on a more expensive drink. It works. It is suggestive selling. McDonald's uses this method all the time. Get the juices flowing. Again, remember hard head soft mouth. You are thinking PROFIT, but to them you are meeting their desire or need. And for those who are non-alcoholic drinkers, I say, "We offer rasp-berry ice-tea as well as regular." (Raspberry being just a little more expensive, but very desirable, again more PROFIT).

I know this sounds cold and seems like I am tak-ing advantage of the customer, but then again, I am teaching you to sell and the secret to making extra money for you and for the company. The better service you give the customers, the more they like the food and the more they think they are getting something special. And the bigger the bill; the bigger the tip. The customer has a GREAT EAT-ING EXPERIENCE, the company has more PROFIT, you get bigger TIPS, and we are all HAPPY.

That is just one example of how it works when you know the product well. Just for the record, I usually work Thursday nights. I have customers that I call regulars. They come in and ask for me. I know their names, I know their foods, and I know their drinks. They are convinced they are special (and they are). I remember if they are left-handed or if they like extra cheese…they DO NOT have to ask. Again, caring is the name of the game and by the way I get extra tips from them. IT WORKS. And when I can, I try to acknowledge the tip by looking them right in the face and saying "Thanks so much, please come back and ask for me, I'm Teddy". That makes them feel special and I now have a regular.

As a side—last week I was waiting on a customer. After she was done eating and done paying the bill, she said, "May I ask you a personal question?" I answered, "sure". She said, "Did you ever sell jewelry?" I answered "Yep, 18 years ago. Why?"

"Well," she said, "I recognized you. I was at one of your shows. You still have the same smile and the same personality. I really liked you then and I like you now. You are very good at pleasing people." All I could say was, "Thanks." But how nice for me, to be remembered 18 years later. I was very rewarded by this customer.

KNOW THE COMPUTER

Knowing the computer systems in your line of sales work is another means of Product Knowledge. You need to have the computer applications in your head so that when the customer does say yes to a sales pitch, you are able to get right on the computer and take the information without any problems. If the computer is off line or if you have trouble processing your application, it gives the customer time for buyer's remorse.

Let me give you an example of what irritates a customer and sets them up with NOT being able to sell or cross sell them any other product. Have a customer come into the bank and make a deposit and ask for their balance. The teller says, "the system is down right now, so I can't give you your balance, but it will be available tomorrow". The hair on the back of the head of the customer is now up – and then you say – "We offer online banking for your convenience if you would like to check your balance at home later tonight". There is no way the customer even heard you – he is still quietly angry that the system is down AGAIN.

Any other time, that might have been a good cross-sale. The convenience of "at home" would be perfect so they could see the account. But right now it is not meeting their need. The customer wants his balance. Do you see what I mean about processing being easy? This is such a common problem. An easy answer is to just say,

"I'm sorry" and then shut up. Sometimes the "feel, felt, found theory" works. "Mr. Customer, I know how you feel, I have felt that same frustration just recently at Penney's, but I found this a common problem when computers are a necessity." Or you might add a flighty remark like computers are great when they work. Otherwise they are annoying. This allows the customer to relate to YOUR frustration and not be so angry. He's been there. This makes us all human.

Have you ever been at the grocery store and the check out clerk can't process the customer in front of you and you stand in line and you wait and wait. You keep looking at your own grocery cart. As time goes on, you begin to question some of your items, like the candy bar you picked up in the check out aisle. Now you have time to decide to put it back. Buyer's remorse is the salespersons enemy. Time to think is wonderful if they are figuring out how to pay for something, but too much time, can also undo all the good thinking. This must be played carefully. I know I told you that if someone decides they want a new dress and they figure out how to pay for it, nothing can undo it. But if they wait in line too long to pay for the dress, the earrings they also picked up may go back since they now have time for buyer's remorse. Too much time can justify the wrong decision for us. So you don't want to antagonize the customer with computer problems or make them wait too long. Processing the sale must be kept an easy process, no matter what the procedure.

I have a friend that is a dance instructor. She was trying to order costumes for the recital. She called three different companies. She got answering machines, recordings, or responses like dial #2 if you wish to place your order. She had one question and could find no one to help her. The one company that had a receptionist answer the phone is the one company where she ordered all 36 costumes. She didn't care if they were more expensive or not, she just wanted service. I think this is a perfect example of keeping the process easy in order to sell your product.

Back to product knowledge. In order to be the best you can be each day, you must be prepared. Know your product, whether you are a car salesman, a waitress, a banker, or a babysitter. Most corporations or businesses are responsible for this. Let me summarize:

1. **Product knowledge classes, continuing education and motivational workshops should be setup and attended**. so you can be familiar with your own products. This does not mean that you need to memorize everything. It does mean that you need to be able to explain the product quickly, simply and accurately with the aid of your brochures, lists and rates in front of you and be up-to-date. I am a firm believer of <u>CHEAT SHEETS</u>. I learned a long time ago to outline

94

some of the facts and have them on a piece of paper <u>WRITTEN</u> down — so I can quickly see them if I need them. Clear back when I was 21 and selling makeup, I learned to cheat sheet. I put down green eye shadow goes better with brown eyeliner on brown haired girls, etc. Know the features (FACTS) and benefits (BONUSES) of every product. Write them out for yourself and look at them – soon the words about the product will roll out of your mouth, because you KNOW it.

2. **<u>It is OK to say, "I don't know, but I'll find out."</u>** When a customer asks something you are not sure of, don't make up an answer or pretend you know. If it is not in your head or on your cheat sheets, find it. Look it up and intelligently re-approach the customer. This builds integrity. It is OK to be human.

3. **<u>The newest thing is the conference call</u>**...mandatory of course. This is a difficult one. It wastes a lot of time. These calls tend to become brag sessions, rather than information sessions. But technology and time has created this "system". It does get everyone informed at the same time. Myself, I think this is a monster rather than a help. I tended to tune out the speaker, read my emails while on the call and worry about the customer waiting for me. But yet, it was quite a time saver, no travel time and much knowledge could be learned. Everyone hears the same thing. And it is the new system, so I certainly complied. Follow the rules of your company. But, honestly, I prefer emails where I can get the same information and read it at my convenience. But then again, I am a visual type

person, I like to see the words...I remember them better. Some people function just as well listening to the phone call and others need to have actual hands on to remember. That's what makes us different but not wrong.

4. **Read all brochures.** Concerning your product and be sure that you have them available for the customer. Know them from cover to cover. Think about Mary Kay Cosmetics, they use brochures as their main tool. They do that so the women can SEE the product. The same technique is used with Tupperware, Pampered Chef. In fact about 80% of Avon's business is from their brochures. Today people are too busy to have others in their homes, so book parties have become the way to do it. Many of the candle companies are doing it this way as well. You need to know each page and product of the brochures because the customer asks about a product- by-product number or by page number. This works for them, so you want to be the one that is the best in giving them service. If you know what they are talking about immediately, they think of you as the expert. That leads to closing the sale. Right?   And don't forget that eBay and other computer sales are also out there, causing you more competition.

5. **Know your computer and the computer processing**. (I've said this three times now). Knowing product is important, but being able to input it is even more important. For example if you are selling an investment, or an insurance product, all information needs to be inputted in front of the customer. If you fumble with the computer

or complain about it, the customer feels uncomfortable. It has to be second nature, like you are handwriting an application. This seems to be a very awkward procedure, but most insurance companies now require an upload of the application rather than the old method of mailing it or faxing it. I have watched an insurance agent in my home with his laptop, struggle thru the application and the electronic signatures. Beads of sweat hit his head, and his embarrassment was obvious as he completed the process. You do NOT want to be in that position. Turn it around because the computer can also be a huge aid for you during the sales pitch. You can pull up comparisons, graphs, slides, interest rates, newspaper articles, and anything else that can be helpful for you to pitch your product. Too much of this, however, can be overwhelming to the customer, so **DON'T OVERSELL**.

*"**It's better to have the philosophy to out-think your competition than outspend them.**" Les Wolff*

It is also important to **know the competitors product**, because you can be sure in this new world of computers, your customers have checked out the internet. He has researched all of the companies and prices himself, it kind of reminds you of a test. The customer can put you on the spot if you are not knowledgeable of your own and the others. For example: In the insurance world it is best to give them options. DO NOT ADVISE. If you would sell the wrong thing and the customer has an accident and are not covered correctly, you are the one liable.

6. **You need to be rehearsed**. The next best thing to selling your product is the cross-sell. If you are selling a new car, you want to up sell the heated seats, the moon-roof, etc. If you are in the food service, you need to suggest a wine, or an appetizer. If you are banking, you want to add the debit card and hopefully a saving account to the checking. You know what I am trying to say here. So knowledge of every product comes to play. I suggest strongly that you role-play. Or at least think scenarios in your head. Practice speaking. Use a tape recorder to help you. Think the beginning, the middle and the end. This will all help you to be more knowledgeable about what you are saying.

7. **Say what you mean and mean what you say"** This applies in all walks of life. When you speak to your children, say what you feel you need to tell them and mean it. If they are to eat all of their dinner, that does not mean half. If they have to be in bed at 8, that does not mean 8:30. The same applies in sales. No matter what you tell the customer, it **BETTER BE THE TRUTH.** Do not make up anything extra just to make the sale. It will come back to haunt you. **Say what you mean,** "This cell phone is guaranteed", and **mean what you say,** "Here is your personal guarantee; please put it somewhere you can find it. Thanks."

8. **BE NICE along the way.** Remember, you are either wasting your time, or investing your time. You are either wasting their time or investing their time. Your decision. **Listen compassionately.** Hear their questions. Answer their questions. YOU be

the expert. KNOW what you are saying. Be honest...kind...informative...knowledgeable...and fair and you will be giving your best. That's all that can be expected. You will be surprised at how this works.

9. **Don't forget the "hard head soft mouth" thinking**. Don't assume the close. Don't assume the objective. Don't talk too much. Be sure to let the customer divert to stories and exchanges of their life. Be kind and help them. Then get back to business. Product knowledge helps because you can relate a situation back to a solution your particular product may solve. Example: customer says that they have to pick up their daughter at school at 3:00. This is a daily routine. You can say, "How old is she? What is her name? Does she like school?" Get personal. Let them know you care. Then say, "How nice for you that you have the time to do that, if something would cause you not to be able to do that, what do you think it would cost for your husband to hire someone to do this everyday?" And then off to the life insurance product. A good way to start the close for life insurance for a woman is with a price quote. Sometimes as they think about their child, they realize how important this can be. I hope you understand what I am saying here. I am a compassionate person, but I also realize at this time that I am here to do a job. I truly believe in my product and know this would help her, not hurt her and at this point I know she needs the product. I am hoping, in the back of my head, that she also knows she needs the product. What usually happened to me (and I was top life insurance sales for 3 years in a row) was that the price

quote for a woman's life policy was far less than she thought it would be and she now feels special thinking she is worth that value. Once convinced even her husband can't talk her out of it or she will feel he doesn't see her worth as a mother. This is a GREAT CARING SALE.

Dealing with the man's coverage isn't as easy, since it is more expensive, but a great line here that sometimes puts them thinking correctly is one my friend uses in her insurance agency when dealing with the woman who has control of the finances: "If we bury your husband, we bury his pay check"...Julie Dale.

10. <u>REMEMBER CALL BACKS DON'T WORK</u>. SELL IT NOW"!!! That's why I like to have both spouses together. The biggest rebuttal I faced was, "I need to talk it over with my husband or wife". If they are together, there is nothing they are going to know tomorrow that they do not know today. You can tell them that directly but nicely with your hard head soft mouth technique.

The only other thing I want to impress on you is that each time a customer comes in or you pick up the phone, a sale is made. Either you sell them or they sell you. I personally would rather be the seller rather than the sellee. The simple fact is that if you can sell, you can sell no matter the product. <u>The product is second to your technique</u>. Not unimportant, but second.

Product knowledge should come at the exact time. Usually after you have established yourself and your company and after you have made conversation, you will discover the need. Then you talk product.   Understand that most of sales is not a canned pitch, but conversation. Don't get me wrong; you must have an idea what you are going to say. An outline of a sales pitch and practice practice practice helps. Be prepared with three feasible options with the middle option being the usual compromise.

(Let me tell you a story, I did a role-play when I went to Chicago for Whittle and Hanks White Paper Sales and they videoed me. I learned so much from them, but the MAJOR thing I got out of it was that I was always biting my nails when I was not speaking. I sure looked like a dummy. I didn't realize how much I put that one fingernail in my mouth. Sounds silly, but I wondered how that looked to the customers.   From that video, I became aware of this action and with much concentration, I stopped it.) My point: Role playing and videotaping can help you.

My last comment on Product Knowledge in this chapter is for you to be careful not to fumble here. You are supposed to be the one that knows it all. It is OK to say I don't know, or I will find out for you. That does not mean you are fumbling or not the expert. It is when you hem and haw around that causes the uneasiness. You want this part to go smoothly because it is the timing that counts here; it is the lead up to the close.

All this adds up to good sales; introduction, conversation, features, benefits, product knowledge and your incentive, with your own technique. Add a smile and warmth and caring and be NICE...listen to the customer, be pleasant and hear what they say. The old rule "LISTEN FOR THE NEED, AND

THEN SELL IT" applies here. No matter the product, no matter the company, product knowledge is important, it helps set everything up. Technique and personality, however sells it. Because you ARE selling YOURSELF first, then the product.

One more thought for you, if this doesn't work with this customer, you probably did nothing wrong. Just go on to the next customer.

People don't plan to fail, they
fail to plan"...Zig Ziglar

V. THE CLOSE

Simply said, the close is the sale. The sale is the service, no matter the product. And it happens within one minute. If you don't close, you don't have a sale. I learned this quickly when I was on the phones selling pens and lighters. I once had a customer tell me "You are very good at this." I answered, "Not good enough, I haven't made the sale." I missed it. I over talked, I over stated the product, I misstated the amount for his need, I missed his leads, and I didn't hear him when he was ready. I missed the sale all together, BUT I WAS GOOD AT IT. Not good enough. So I went on to the next call, I learned from it, I didn't dwell on it. But you need to be aware there is timing in closing. The customer will let you know when they are ready, and if you don't recognize this sign, you will continue talking 'til you talk them out of it. That's a fact!

Let me remind you, you can have all the personality in the world, you can have all your techniques down pat, you can be a hard seller or a soft seller, you can be happy or sad; but in the end, if you don't' close, you don't have a sale.

Once again, closing is timing. You must be ready for it at any time. If it comes early in the informational talk, "go for it". If you have to fight for it, then fight and then "go for it."

Your soft mouth helps, but your hard head counts. Your head has to remember the bottom dollar. A sale is only good if it makes money for all concerned and if it meets the needs of the customer while you are making money. Don't compromise on cost for a sale, they will feel this and not buy. You can barter but be careful. Remember the customer wants everything for nothing. They know the game.

So you need to be smart enough to stop the game at a good profit. Sometimes it really is money that matters to them. I have a friend that used to say, "How do you want to pay for this -cash, credit card or green stamps?" It was often just enough to lighten up the customer to get the job done.

Some very important rules here that apply to the Close.

1. **YOU MUST ASK FOR THE SALE** – it just doesn't happen. BUT YOU MUST KNOW WHEN TO ASK.

2. After you have presented your close and have asked for the sale, you must be quiet. **"Silence is golden".**

THE FIRST ONE TO SPEAK LOSES

I know that sounds hard, but it is true. When you state a strong point, shut up. The first one to speak after that loses. Sometimes you must stay quiet while they are thinking. Thinking how to get out of it, thinking how much they need it, thinking how much they want it, thinking how they are going to pay for it. When they get all this thinking straight, they will acknowledge you. If they speak a question or a rebut, then you KNOW they are interested. They didn't say NO. Answer their questions intelligently and honestly, and be quiet again. If they say OK or simply nod with a smile. Then respond with "Let's get started with your name, address, etc.

I want to confide in you and tell you this is a hard one for me. I am an impatient human being and I often lose this one. I have to force myself to wait it out. You see if you wait it out, then the customer can't come back with a question that you can't answer, or acknowledge, or at least find the answer to it. But if you speak first, you lose. More often than not, you will say something that you THINK they are concerned about and blow the whole closing timing. If they have questions or rebuts, answer them and close again. Ask again for the business, and then again be quiet.

You are not done when the sale is completed. More conversation is needed to relax the customer and you make appreciation statements. Smile and thank them. Thank them on your behalf and on the behalf of your business. Tell them you will help them any way they need. Be sure they are completely satisfied. Reiterate all the facts and confirm what has taken place. Ask if they have any questions. Better to resolve everything now. Best to do it all right in the first place. Restate what they purchased. This often leads to cross sales. I had a habit of always telling them "Please feel free to call me anytime, I am here to help you. I can service you and all your needs, that is what I do best." Be sincere and pleased and proud of them. Being proud of them makes them feel they made a good choice. If possible setup a follow-up appointment right then. Having your planner handy makes it easy for you and them. It makes them feel you are saving them the hassle of having to call you next week.

Be sure to clean everything up, give them all the receipts and brochures that went with the sale. Put all papers in a nice folder, with your business card and include your email address and tell them you are happy to receive emails. Be sure they understand your hours and that you will come to their home or them to your office at their convenience. If they can't make a follow up right then, Ask them to please call for an appointment so you can have everything ready for them and that in itself sets up professionalism. Tell them you look forward to hearing from them. Make them feel very important to you and you want to have time just for them.

Experience is knowing a lot of things you shouldn't do"...William S. Knudsen

AFTER THE CLOSE

After the close, and you are back at the office update your x-file so you can remember details about this customer. Mark your calendar to call them or email them in approximately a week to 10 days to see if everything is OK. Example: When I sold a checking account, I would call to see if they got their checks and if they were correct. This gave me a chance to talk with them further on other things. Remain honest and caring and enthusiastic – don't let down after the sale. I view that as you winning a customer and not just a sale.

Write down the little things, number of children, their ages, names, hobbies, etc.; so when they call in or email you, you will remember them. You can then go to the file and relate to them. And they will remember you and they think you are special. They think you THINK they are special. So you will have to remember this in order to keep it all straight. I don't know about you, but this is not easy, but it is personal and caring and keeping it special is **ONE OF THE SECRETS TO SELLING**.

In conclusion remember to be yourself, be unique, use your personality and technique. Give your best to every customer and the company or your own business. Focus on what is important.

If you keep in mind that the business and the customer come first, then the rest is easy.

I can't quite quit here, although I do suppose you wish I were done. I have one shorter chapter.

"Treat everyone fairly, but not necessarily the same"

VI. THE FOLLOW UP

It is this area that I excel. I called customers to see if they were happy with their checks, and then cross-sold them.   I called customers to see if they enjoyed their meal, made a new reservation for the next weekend. If they had a problem; I called to be sure everything got solved. I checked on their house closings and their child's birthday party they mentioned. I called just to thank them or to tell them, "I really enjoyed meeting you" and they believed me and I meant it because in my head I HAD made a friend. Ultimately I became THEIR insurance agent, THEIR banker, and THEIR personal waitress. They felt I became loyal to them and they to me. Follow up is of the utmost importance. It confirms the company. It confirms you. It makes the customer know he is special. He becomes attached to you. It makes the customer call you "MY" insurance agent, "MY" banker, "MY" teacher, MY friend.

This action, the follow-up, confirms my secret. It is what makes my method special. I put some of the obligation back on them to make a decision, to continue to allow me to sell them with my hard head and soft mouth method. I allow them to accept my kindness and friendship and see my heart as I see theirs. And we are all happy.

Selling is a simple process. Listen to the customer, listen for the need, find the need and meet the need. In other words, hear what they want and sell it to them. This can all be accomplished with a logical head, wanting the sale, wanting PROFIT, using kind but firm words, balancing your thinking and being that rare person that can take care of hearts while taking care of business.

You have just become a successful salesperson. Hopefully everyone is happy; the customer, your business or company, your superior and YOU. It is a simple system and it's my method.

I call it **SIMPLIFIED $ALES**. The end.

PERSONAL NOTE TO MY READERS

"I am what I am"...Popeye

Dear Readers:

The book is complete. It is a simple book. I hope and pray that it helped you. My goal was to make you the best you are with some simple rules and a heart.

If I helped you with one thing in life, if I helped you with one extra sale, if I helped you feel better about yourself just once; then I will have accomplished what I set out to do. I start my book out with ***"If you always do what you always did, you will always get what you always got."*** I hope this book helped you to make some changes so you can be successful and happy; while considering the hearts along the way.

Thank you for reading my book.

Teddy Behrendt

Teddy Behrendt
Comments: teddy_behrendt_804@comcast.net

"You are what you are and where you are because of what has gone into your mind. You can change who-what-where you are by changing what goes on in your mind."...Anonymous

About the Author

Teddy Behrendt is a retired Assistant Vice President, Branch Manager in the banking industry. She has 22 years of banking experience, 20 years of speaking and training, and 12 years of insurance; all of which included sales. She is known as the sales "guru" and "cheerleader. Being diversified in all types of sales, having owned her own business, worked on commission and being salaried all contributed to the contents of this book. She is fun, dynamic and loud. (At least that's what her employees told her). The biggest asset Teddy has is her abundance of energy. She contributes her success to loving God, loving her wonderful family of daughters and grandchildren, and her positive attitude handed down to her from her Mom. Teddy lives in Sterling, IL. and welcomes any communication. Please contact her to schedule a Teddy Behrendt Simple Sales Workshop or a motivational speech.

Teddy Behrendt
815-441-5389
teddy_behendt_804@comcast.net

6125509R0

Made in the USA
Charleston, SC
17 September 2010